THE SECOND ALPHA HEIR

C.L. LEDFORD

CONTENTS

PROLOGUE

Have you ever had to grow up in the shadow of an older sibling? Well, I did, and it sucks. Not only did I not measure up to him in size, but I was not well-liked within my pack either. My entire life of being picked on and bullied by my peers became normal for me since I wasn't big enough nor strong enough, even though my status should have kept them from bullying me.

My name is Nolen, and I'm the second son to the leaders, the Alpha, and Luna of the Rhyolite pack.

Being born small, everyone called me the runt of the litter. My brother Archer would be the next Alpha of the pack once he finished up his Alpha training. My father, the Alpha, had been training him since he could walk. He'd started to train me, but when it appeared that I would not be as agile as Archer, he just let me do my own thing.

So there I was, at the edge of the roof, looking down at the pack walking around below me. The lush green forest of the Cairn surrounded us as I glanced over it from my spot. This was my favorite spot to get away from the rest of them. That way, no one could bully me. They wouldn't dare bully me around Archer because he was the next in line to become alpha and they wanted to stay in his good graces. He'd been trying to train me to fight, but it wasn't going anywhere.

Archer continued to push me to be better, even when I was crawling on the ground to move away from him. You see, I wasn't built like my brother. I was thirteen years old and as scrawny as a sewing needle, and I'd been told I hit like a girl.

I didn't know what girls they were fighting, but I knew for sure that I didn't punch like some of the girls in my class. Those girls packed a wallop, and I tried to stay away from them. I was only five foot eight inches, but my mother kept telling me that I would grow taller as I aged. She liked to console me when she thought I was depressed, but I could care less; it didn't hurt anymore.

"NOLEN!"

The sound of my mother's voice calling for me in the house floated up to me. No doubt to tell me I needed to come down off the roof. Like she had told me many times. If she only knew why I came up here. I glanced around and jumped from the roof to the balcony. Making my way through the doors and down the stairs to my mother's office. I stopped at her door and knocked.

"Come in, Nolen,"

My mother stood by her desk talking with my father and my brother. My brother's future Beta and best friend stood beside him, and I slowly made my way to them. My mother smiled at me while my father shot me the same look he'd aimed at me these last three years—one of dissatisfaction that I could not seem to erase from his features. Oh, he loved me, but what he wouldn't do to be blessed with two heirs like Archer. I walked up to her, holding my head up, "Yes, Mother?"

Being only an inch taller than her, I would be considered short for a male wolf, whereas my brother, half a foot taller than me, was giant. My brother grinned at me, but his Beta scowled; I continued to stare at him, and he decided to glance away from me, my rank over him winning out, at least for the time being. I would pay for this stare-down later, because once alone, he would beat me, but at this moment, I found pleasure in making him turn his eyes. You see, since he was beta, he was a step down in rank, even though I wouldn't be the next alpha of the pack.

"Your father and brother have to go to Dolostone pack. I need you to stay close to the packhouse and not go running around." My mother surveyed the others in the room, giving them her mom/luna stare. My mother was technically second in command since she was my father's fated mate and Luna. When my father and his beta left the pack for business, she was the one who kept the pack in line. Not like she had to try hard, as with one of those Luna looks, the pack did whatever she wanted.

I gazed at my father and then my brother; he smiled and winked at me. I turned back to my father, and he came up to me, placing both of his hands on my shoulders. My brother and I took after him in our appearance; both possessing his dark blue eyes and dark hair. My brother got his build, but I don't know if I would ever be built like him. I met his eyes with my own and nodded to him. He smiled at me, and with a nod and a motion of his hand, he, my brother, and the future Beta walked through the office door. Leaving my mother and me there in the room. Since they were taking the beta's son with them, my dad's beta could stay here and help my mother with the pack.

Three weeks passed since my father, brother and the future Beta departed from the pack. Mother showed no concern for them, but something appeared off to me. A week had gone by with none of the usual bullying from my peers. Which was odd in itself because they all loved to make my life miserable every chance they got. Something deep down in my soul felt absent, but each time I brought this up to my mother, she would tell me how ridiculous I sounded.

Sitting in my room reading a book, I heard cars pulling up the drive to the packhouse. I stared out my window and observed that the once polished SUVs now showed signs of deep claw marks down their sides. I spotted my dad getting out of the middle car like always, along with the future Beta Axel. They were both in only shorts, meaning they'd recently shifted to their wolf forms at some point during their trip back. My heart sank when I spotted the blood on their skin, and they snapped the doors shut.

Where is Archer? I thought to myself as worry laced through me. He hadn't gotten out of the vehicle.

Sprinting from my room, I raced down the stairs to where my father stood on the steps outside so that I could find out where my brother was. I had never run that fast through the packhouse in my entire life, and when I got to the front doors, my mother sat on her knees, my brother's body splayed out with his head in her lap.

I sensed time standing still as I stood there in the doorway looking at the scene before me. My heart rate increased at the sight; he wasn't moving and wasn't breathing. She continued to wail in sorrow, pulling him closer to her as she rocked him back and forth. His blood stained the steps and her clothes from the deep gashes on his torso.

My father studied me as I went to my mother and brother. I dropped to my knees beside her, grabbing his limp, cold hand. I couldn't help but cry out, and hot liquid tears bubbled in my eyes as I gaped up at the sky. My brother, who I'd admired all my life, now lay there lifeless because some other wolf took him from my family and me. Unable to believe that he no longer lived among us, anger rose inside of me. Why would the Moon

Goddess do this to me, to my family, when we had been loyal to her our entire existence?

What would happen now that Archer, the heir, went to be with the Moon Goddess? I looked back at my father, tears streaming down my face. He just stood there as more of the pack ran up to the packhouse after hearing my mother and my yell of anguish. The howls in the distance told me that the entire pack now realized that the next Alpha had passed into the heavens.

CHAPTER ONE: ALPHA TRAINING

Two weeks after my brother's funeral, I made my way north to the Quartzite pack with my mother and father. Since the funeral, no one had messed with me; I was primarily ignored. I sat in the middle SUV, glancing out the window as we rode by the lush fields of flowers and trees. They all looked dull since he'd left.

I hated that they had killed him. If anything, it should have been me—no one would have minded if I'd died, being nothing to the pack but a disgrace. Archer, though, had kept them together and made them proud. He would have led them until his heir took over, and so forth.

We pulled up to the wrought-iron gates of my father's friend's pack, and the two massive wolves guarding it let us pass with a nod of their head. The packhouse stood about the same size as my pack's, and its tall white columns and stone sides looked like they gleamed in the sunshine. The first-floor windows took up the entire height of the first floor.

I caught sight of the massive Alpha and his beautiful Luna standing on the river stone steps waiting for us, his son and daughter stood on either side of them. The Beta stood to the son's left, the Delta stood beside the daughter. They all appeared happy that we were coming, even though I dreaded these four years.

The vehicles all stopped, the wolves in front of our SUV got out, letting me, my mother, and my father out. I glanced around the place, noticing nothing about the area had changed since coming here as a tiny pup, and the Alpha and Beta still scared me. They were still massive, even though I had grown since I was here last.

I walked forward with my parents and recognized the daughter hiding behind the Luna's skirts. I stared at her, and she gave me a tiny grin, but I couldn't reciprocate her smile, which didn't deter her one bit as she sized me up. Her amber eyes took in my appearance before she brought them back up to my eyes. She was cute, but there was no sense getting close to her. I was here to train and hopefully become better than what I was.

"Alpha of Rhyolite, my old friend. I wish this visit could have been under better circumstances," said the Alpha of Quartzite.

"Same, my friend. This is my second son, Nolen. He has grown some since you last saw him."

"Ah, you cannot deny him if you wanted to. He is the spitting image of you,"

My father gazed back at me, and his eyes held something never before seen in them when he looked at me. My mother brought me closer to her side, and I knew she did not want to let me out of her sight. I didn't see much of our resemblance since he was so much bigger.

"Well, come in, we will have a feast and then get him into a room. Nolen, this is my Delta, his name is Eric, and he will be the first part of your training. My Beta, Adam, will help you strengthen yourself," Alpha Roman told me as he came up to me and placed his arm around my shoulders, leading me into the packhouse and away from my parents, "Don't let your father fool you; I have known him for years, and he was just as scrawny as you at this age."

I glanced back at my father and mother, and I could have sworn I caught him rolling his eyes as my mother smiled. I had not seen her smile since my brother passed. I continued with the Alpha, and his son came up to my other side and nudged me.

I looked over at the sandy-blonde boy beside me, whose muscles bulged a little more on him than mine, but he looked friendly enough. His green eyes shone against the tawny color skin of his skin. "We'll be training together. We're going to make our packs the best of the best when we take over."

I nodded, thinking that this alpha heir was going to kick my ass in the training ring.

At dinner, the Quartzite pack and I were introduced, and they all applauded me and wished me well in my training. I met the Delta's daughter and his wife, along with Beta Adam's mate, who was heavy with pup. I sat without speaking to anyone while my father and Alpha Roman talked. I couldn't help but notice that the Alpha's daughter kept glancing over at me. She started to make me feel uneasy since no girl had ever paid much attention to me at my own pack.

Learning the tiny pup approached her tenth birthday unnerved me, her being three years younger than me and already giving me more interest than others at Rhyolite. I continued to keep my head down until Sawyer, the heir to the Quartzite pack, came up and sat next to me.

"So, Nolen, what do the girls look like at your pack?" he inquired as he tore into his plate of steak, potatoes, and corn.

"I wouldn't know," I told him, my eyebrows furrowed.

Sawyer gave me a look of surprise, his fork halfway to his mouth, "What! You are an alpha, they should be falling at your feet."

I kept my eyes on my plate while putting more potatoes in my mouth and swallowing, "I'm nothing in the pack's eyes. They worshipped my brother."

"Why, because you haven't come into your own yet? I mean, you could have been training your body before now, but that can be remedied." Sawyer chuckled as he shoveled food into his mouth. This wolf was blunt. I didn't know if I liked that or not. He kind of reminded me of Archer.

I shook my head as a few of the girls from his pack strolled by the table, their eyes sizing me up, but they didn't linger on me. Their eyes went to Sawyer, and he seemed to relish their attention. His mannerisms were exactly like my brother, girls falling at his feet without him even trying.

"So, what kind of training have you had?" Sawyer continued to question me in between bites.

"Not much, since I wasn't going to be next in line. Besides, no one would want me as Alpha anyway," I told him, finishing up my plate of food.

"Well, tomorrow is going to be fun then!" he exclaimed, his eyes shining in delight.

I rolled my eyes and groaned; how could any of this be fun? In the past, when Archer would wake me up at four in the morning, I could hardly stay up the rest of the day. Now I would be living the life intended for him. I surveyed the pack as they sat there enjoying their meal. *How many of them have lost a loved one?* I wondered. I realized that even though I would not like my life over the next few years, I needed to get strong enough to kill the wolf who took my brother away from my family.

I would become an Alpha that Archer would be proud of.

)))) 🐺 (((((

When the knock came upon my door that morning, nothing would prepare me for what awaited me. I pulled on my shirt, jogging pants, and running shoes and went downstairs. Sawyer met me in the dining room, where we sat across from each other. An Omega brought two plates of food and glasses of water to us. The meal was kind of bland; nevertheless, I ate it.

"Beta Adam doesn't want us upchucking as he runs us to death," Sawyer mumbled with a mouth full of toast. I grunted, not fully awake yet, dreading what lay before me. The moon still sat in the sky when we finished our food. We both headed out, and I spotted Beta Adam standing out on the steps with his back turned, waiting for us.

"Next time, you both need to be out here before me; if not, you will run two laps more around the pack lands," Beta Adam instructed, turning to face us, "and if it continues, another lap will be added each day. This is your first and last warning."

That woke me up. If this pack's territory compared to anything like mine, it was huge. I shared a glance with Sawyer, and he seemed just as surprised as me.

"Now that I have your attention, pups, this is how our morning routine is going to work. You will wake up, have breakfast, and be out here before me. If not, you now understand the consequences; then we will run until I cannot run any longer. Once we are finished running, we will strength train; after that, you will have lunch. After lunch is your studies with Delta Eric. For the first few weeks, you will meet me out here three days a week. You will meet me the other two days at the training fields, where you both will spar until I see improvement. Are we clear?" Beta Adam questioned us, his eyes shifting between ours. This wolf was intimidating. I couldn't believe he was a Beta.

Sawyer and I both nodded, "Yes, sir, Beta Adam."

I noted the slight grin on his lips, and then it faded. He nodded, jogged down the steps, and we followed him. I hoped that I would at least be able to keep up with him. Otherwise, I was sure that he would make me run more laps.

By the time Beta Adam got tired, Sawyer and I were gasping for breath. We'd stayed together and never stopped running, but this damn pack land was bigger than I thought. Much bigger than ours, that was for sure. Stooped over his hands on his knees, Sawyer tried to catch his breath. It took everything in me to keep upright, and I crossed my arms over my head to extend my lungs better. Sweat poured off me in places I didn't know it could leave the body.

Beta Adam stood there a moment before he motioned us forward, and I dared not make a sound as he led us over to a building. Once inside, he assigned us to different machines. He put me on a simple stand-alone with a long barbell rod. I sat down at it, and he put twenty pounds on each side. I peered up at him, afraid that I would disappoint him even with this light of weights.

Beta Adam stared down at me, a take-no-shit expression on his face. "This is lighter than you should be lifting at your age. You have till the end of the week to increase to more than this."

I started curling the forty pounds, and I continued to push myself until I couldn't any longer. He switched us often to different machines. We continued to change devices until noon, when he stopped us, and we went to lunch. My whole body hurt, and I had never been pushed that hard, even by my brother.

The next day, we started sparring training, but I didn't see that going any better than the prior morning. We sat down at the table that evening to eat.

"You guys stink!" a female voice came from behind us. I turned around and saw the Delta's daughter and a few other she-wolves behind her cover their noses with their hands while they scrunched their foreheads in disgust. I peered over at Sawyer, watching as he rose from the table and started to chase after her. She screamed, which brought attention to them both as he caught her and wrapped her up in his arms to carry her back to the table.

"Sawyer! Put me down! I'm now going to have to take another bath! Sawyer!"

"Now, now, Danika, is that how you talk to an Alpha?" he taunted her. She growled, and he chuckled loudly. He sat her between us and then started to eat. She kept her hand over her nose, and I couldn't help but chuckle at her face. The other she-wolves seemed disappointed that he'd raced after her, but they went to their regular table to sit, leaving Danika between us.

"You both really need to take a shower before going to my dad." Her voice had changed since she held her nose closed, trying to keep from smelling us

"Yeah, perhaps we do." I could smell myself. Getting up, Danika let out the breath that she'd held in her lungs.

I put my plate in the dirty bin and made my way back to my room. I stripped out of the joggers, t-shirt, and underwear and climbed into the shower. The hot water felt amazing on my sore muscles. I stood there under the steaming water before grabbing a loofa and body wash; I slathered it onto my body, making the muscles I never knew were there scream with every movement. Rinsing off, I grabbed the bar of soap and used it to wash my face.

Stepping out of the shower, I dried off, put on some fresh clothes, and headed back to Delta Eric's office. As I walked down the stairs, the Alpha's daughter sat on the steps, her head in her lap. I started to walk past her, but something pulled me to her. I stopped and watched her for a while before sitting beside her. "Hey, you, okay?"

She peeked up at me, her amber eyes red and puffy. I grinned at her, and she smiled sadly back at me. Her eyes pulled me into them while tears clung to her eyelashes. Her lashes were the longest things my eyes had ever gazed upon. She shook her head and laid it in her lap again. Her body shook as she quietly sobbed. I didn't know what to do for her, so I just sat there for a moment, looking around. A group of boys sat in a circle near a corner, their backs to us as they laughed and cut up with each other. Turning back to face her, I raised my eyebrow, questioning her. "Can I do anything?"

She glanced back at me with a slight hiccup. Her eyes seemed to brighten at my offer. She pointed over to the group of boys. "Can you get my dolly back from them?"

I nodded and got up from the steps; as I went up to them, I noticed they started cutting the doll's hair and were drawing on its arms and face. One boy laughed, and I grabbed the doll from him, he turned with a growl before seeing who I was, and it died on his lips. He and the other boys lowered their eyes and bared their necks to me. Taken aback by this show of submission, I stood there for a moment, before I fixed my face and glared at them. "Is there a reason you took her doll from her?"

They all stayed silent until the one who'd growled at me spoke up, "It was all in good fun, Nolen. We didn't plan to do all of this."

I growled at him, and he whimpered. I didn't know where the noise came from. This was not how I acted at my pack. I was never this sure of myself. "So, taking a little girl's doll. A girl that deserves your respect because she is of alpha blood, is all in good fun because she's littler than all of you?"

"No, sir. We are sorry, it won't happen again. We promise," another boy piped up, his eyes filled with tears as he glanced up at me.

"Since you defaced her doll, I expect you to buy her another one by the end of the week to pay for the one you destroyed."

"Yes, sir," they chanted to me and ran off down the hall of the packhouse and through the doors. There could be repercussions for my actions, but at the moment, I didn't care.

I turned and went back to her. She gazed up at me, and once she spotted the doll in my hand gave me the impression that she would cry again, tears building up in her beautiful eyes. Kneeling in front of her, I held out the doll, giving her a grin. "Hey, don't worry, I told them they needed to replace it."

She gawked at me with those breathtaking amber eyes, and then she smiled, lunging into me as she wrapped her arms around my neck. I stood there, stunned at first, but it felt right as I enfolded her tiny body with my arms.

CHAPTER TWO: VOICES

Four in the morning rolled around quicker than expected, and I got up, pulling my joggers and tank shirt on. I had been here about two months now and was capable of running quicker than Beta Adam, almost as fast as Sawyer, and I lifted more than Sawyer now.

I made my way to the dining room and sat down. An omega sat the same bland food and water down before me, and I thanked him and began eating. Sawyer came down a few moments later and plopped down in front of me. Another omega brought him a plate, and he mumbled something that sounded like 'thank you.'

I finished my food and water, took my plate and cup to the dirty bin, walked out of the room, and made my way to the porch. Beta Adam approached the steps, and as his scent wafted to me I glanced over my shoulder, hoping Sawyer got here soon because I didn't want to run an extra two laps this morning.

Feeling great in my skin and more confident now that I'd started showing more definition, Beta Adam was proud of my progress. I had impressed Delta Eric as well since I started with him after being late due to helping the Alpha's daughter, Amora.

I hadn't tried to make an excuse and told him that it wouldn't happen again. He hadn't questioned me, which I thought was weird. So, I'd gone with it. I had sat down beside Sawyer, and he'd seemed to be sniffing me the entire time. He kept giving me looks but finally chilled out. The Delta's class had gone by pretty quickly that day, but it'd become more challenging each week.

Just as the Beta's scent became more potent, Sawyer came out the front doors. I sighed, knowing we had barely escaped being punished. I glanced at him, and he appeared to have woken up more since I saw him in the dining room. Sawyer had become another person that I looked up to; he wasn't like the other ranks in my pack, but he also hadn't known me for most of my life. These four years were sure to be torture if Sawyer and I hadn't become friends.

Sawyer started to stretch as he peered over to me, "Hey, dude, how did you sleep last night? Want to go to a party tomorrow with me?"

"Party? Are you sure?" I had never been invited to a party. It shouldn't have been a surprise, as the wolves here didn't treat me like my pack did, but it was always in the back of my mind that it might be a trick.

Sawyer cocked his head to the side as he stared at me with a smirk while he continued to stretch. "Yeah, me and a few of the warriors always go to this human's parties, and we kinda just crash it. But they don't care. The girls love it when we come around."

"I'll think about it," I told him as I began to stretch. My muscles were loose, and they gave me added weight. The training had really bulked me out.

"My sister talks about you a lot." I turned to him and stared at him. My heart started to accelerate at the mention of his sister. Sawyer stood back up, giving me one of his knowing grins.

He didn't like his sister to be around the un-mated males, and being three years younger than me, I truly believed she was as much my sister as she was his. I took a deep breath, waiting for him to say something else on the subject. When he didn't, I figured he wanted me to ask him why, so I indulged. "Why would she be talking about me?"

"Because you're her new 'knight in shining armor' now. You did make that group of boys buy her another doll, right?"

"That happened two months ago," I told him with a shrug, giving him a wary look. My heart wouldn't slow down, which made me start to sweat.

He laughed and then turned away from me. Being only a few months older than me, Sawyer would shift and turn eighteen before I left. I would be at his pack to witness it since I would still be living with them for a few more months after his birthday. But he had been on a whole other level in his training. I was almost to his level, but Beta Adam still thought I needed just a little bit more.

The first time we'd sparred, he'd kicked my ass. But I had continued to get back up, which gave me the impression that was what made Beta Adam push me harder than what he had been. Bloodied and bruised for weeks after those first two days that week, we'd fought until we couldn't fight any longer. I had kept pushing myself to keep getting up even when my body wanted to submit. By the time we both couldn't persuade our bodies to stay upright, half the wolves that were in training had been surrounding us—encouraging us to continue.

Now we were running again for the third time, and I longed for today to turn into Saturday. Beta Adam continued to alter our course each day so it didn't become routine. This morning we were running in the woods where the patrols kept watch. Every once in a while, I saw massive paw print on the trail where the patrols ran to keep the pack safe.

I imagined the freedom when I got to shift into my wolf. The wind in my fur, my paws pounding on the ground, taking me ever forward. Being one with my wolf was one of my dreams that seemed to be more of a reality than a mate. My future mate's rejection didn't faze me; this would be my reality, especially in my pack.

A howl sounded through the air, which made me and Sawyer stop. Beta Adam quickly turned to us and listened; another cry came forth, and he came up to us. Holding onto our shoulders as he started mind linking someone. I became nervous; the patrols normally never howled like that unless something entered the territory uninvited. The beta's grip tightened, and I clenched my jaw to keep from letting a yelp out. Seconds went by as he conversed with whoever, then he finally cut the link and his features turned hard.

"Ready yourselves. I realize you can't shift yet, but I need your help. You both are strong enough in human form now. I'm going to shift. I'll be right back," he told us, running into the trees to shift.

We stood on the trail back-to-back, keeping our eyes and ears open, slowing our breathing and our heart rates to keep the enemy from hearing us. Beta Adam made it back to us just as I picked up another wolf's scent. I hadn't met everyone in the pack yet, but I sensed the tension in Sawyer's aura. This meant only one thing—this wolf was no friend. I continued to swivel my head, waiting for them to come out of the underbrush.

The beta's reddish wolf gazed at us and snorted; his eyes went past us as a muddy brown wolf jumped out, snarling and brandishing his teeth. Beta Adam sprang forward and over us, attacking the rogue wolf, while two other wolves appeared and came at Sawyer and me. We pushed off each other and went to the massive beasts before us.

I grabbed the wolf in front of me by his jaws, keeping him at bay as his saliva ran down my arms. He thrashed his teeth, trying to sink them into my flesh. The muscles in my arms flexed and strained as I tried to keep him from tearing into me.

Push harder, Nolen!

The voice in my head startled me, but I used my legs and pushed the wolf up. Grabbing the lower and upper part of his jaws, I pulled with all my strength, tearing his lower jaw from his face. I felt like something else gave me strength; my whole body buzzed with whatever this power was. Turning, Sawyer was putting up a good fight with a grey wolf, and I lunged into the fray with him, grabbing hold of the wolf's neck as Sawyer grabbed his jaw, snapping it. The wolf fell, lifeless, at his feet. I jumped from his body and observed my surroundings, looking for the Beta.

Picking up on the snarling and tearing of skin nearby, I looked to Sawyer, and we both nodded. We ran to the fighting and witnessed Beta Adam combating three wolves, each trying to secure their hold on him to take him down. I slowed my pace at the sight of the four giant wolves fighting each other. The Beta was taller than the others that kept attacking and then retreating. Each wolf had gouges in their skin where blood spilled onto the ground from the wounded flesh.

Faster, Nolen! the voice in my head commanded. I pushed faster, Sawyer accelerating along with me, and we tackled two of the wolves so that Beta Adam could take on the one in front of him. I grappled with the wolf before me, his claws splitting the skin on my chest apart. Blood spilled from the deep canyons, and I went forward, the sensation of a power I had never known before flowing through me.

The wolf withdrew back a little to put distance between us, and I then caught sight of my opportunity when he lunged. As I went under him, the power that rushed through me focused on my right hand as I jerked his vocal cords from his throat. Blood poured out as the wolf fell on top of me; the power that had helped me quickly evaporating, and I didn't possess the strength to push his dead weight off.

The heavy body of the full-grown wolf pressed me into the ground, his blood continuing to spray out. I lay there, thankful I was already down, since the darkness started enveloping me. Beneath the heat of the wolf and smell of blood covering me, I heard people and wolves running toward me.

"Nolen!"

You are one determined pup; we are destined for wonderful things, Nolen.

The feeling of my body being pulled inside out stressed me. I kept trying to move my arms and legs, but they didn't budge. I tried to open my eyes but could not free them. I started to panic, my breathing and heartrate increasing. I thought I was thrashing around but could also tell that my body didn't respond to my brain's request.

Rest, young Alpha. Your body needs to heal. The voice startled me as this mysterious being took up a small portion of my mind. Power surged back into me as this voice spoke.

Who are you? I asked, not entirely understanding why I was talking to something in my head. I was pretty sure if I started to answer myself, I should be committed to a crazy house, but being a werewolf, there was probably no place for that.

You should know, Nolen. Living your whole life among your pack, the voice huffed. Maybe it snorted; I couldn't really tell. But it seemed annoyed with me.

Yes, but I shouldn't be able to hear you till we shift. Why now? I realized that this other voice was my wolf, but there was no way we would be able to communicate until my eighteenth birthday, when we would shift.

Because that's what happens sometimes, it informed me, huffing again in my mind. I tried to make out what its fur was like, but try as I might, I couldn't see it.

What do you mean happens sometimes? And why did it happen now? What's your name? I probed. Interested in finding out more than I already knew.

My name is Sarge. Most of the time, it happens when you need me sooner. Like when those wolves attacked, if I hadn't helped, you wouldn't be here to complete your destiny, he answered.

Destiny. My destiny wouldn't be fulfilled if I had died. But what about Archer's future? His life that he would never get to live, what happened to his mate?

Pleasure to meet you, but why is my life more important than others? Why did my brother have to die? Since you are here now, does that mean we will shift sooner? What about Sawyer? Did he obtain his wolf too? I wanted to know why, and since we were one and the same, he wouldn't be able to hide that answer from me, right?

No, and no, I can only surface on your eighteenth birthday. I'm not sure why your brother had to leave you, Nolen. He whimpered inside my head, sadness flooding through me. Why was he sad? He had never set eyes on my brother. I couldn't take this anymore. I wanted answers, but I didn't think I was ready for them.

Changing the subject from the still open wound of my brother, I tried again to move my arms, but they stayed in place. *Do you know how long we have been out?*

No, because I still need eyes to tell what is going on, like you, he smarted off to me. I shook my head and relaxed; at least I wasn't going to be alone inside my head. While my body healed, I would have some form of company. I didn't know how long I had been out, but I understood if I had to be out any longer, Sarge would be able to give me more information on why he'd showed up early.

You are never alone, Nolen; I've been here waiting to be reborn, Sarge indicated.

Yeah, well, I've felt like it since Archer passed. Sulking as it got quiet again in my head and the slight sense of loneliness returned, I started to drift back off to sleep. Sarge took up residence in the back of my consciousness, curling up, waiting for my body to awaken and be able to move about.

CHAPTER THREE: SCARS

When I came out of the medically induced coma the pack doctor put me in, I felt like a thousand wolves had barreled through me. The pack doctor, Leon, told me he expected me to be out for a few more days, even with Alpha blood running in my veins, awakening this early occurred rarely. He kept me two extra days to be sure my vitals stayed stable. During that time, Sawyer came to see me, and he always made sure it was before he had to run.

"Hey! If I have to be up. You have to be up," he would tell me in-between bites of his light breakfast.

I shook my head, and I knew Sarge laughed in the back of my mind. This would take some getting used to once I left the hospital and rejoined the pack. Today, I would be leaving the pack hospital, which made me happy because these four walls seemed to be closing in on me. I wanted to be able to train and get back into my routine.

The Alpha and Luna had told my parents, and they called me every day once I had awoken to make sure I still lived. It took all the convincing in the world to keep my mother at home. Ever since Archer had passed, she'd become insistent on keeping in touch with me, and now with this incident, she would be even more adamant. I didn't tell her about the scar that showed prominently on my chest, but I was sure the Alpha here told her. Several nice deep craters over the left side of my chest would be with me till my death.

Grimacing, I slid my shirt over my head, and the motion pulled on the new skin forming over my chest. "How was the party?"

"Oh, I didn't go. I wanted to show you around, to show you a good time. Some of the other younger wolves convinced my dad into throwing you a recovery party," he laughed as he finished his meal.

Sawyer is an Alpha too. His wolf is at the edge as well. I can feel his aura, Sarge said to me, and I peered at him out of the corner of my eye.

I rolled my eyes. *Yes, he's an Alpha. What made you think he wasn't?*

Nothing made me think that. He will be beneficial to us; he is part of our destiny, Sarge told me; I could see him more in my mind's eye but not enough to reveal his coat color.

I turned and grabbed my small bag that had my shredded clothes in it. I should have told them to throw them away. It's not like I would be wearing them anymore. I sat down in one of the chairs and watched Sawyer down the rest of his water.

It helped when he came around; I had Sarge but having Sawyer there to tell me how things were going during training was exciting. He would complain about not having me there to take some of Beta Adam's punishment, and I would laugh at him because it would have been worse if I had been there.

"Isn't it about time for you to be sparring?"

Sawyer turned to me with one of his shit-eating grins, "And who am I supposed to be sparring? My sparring partner is still in the hospital."

"So, what are you going to do?"

"I don't have a fucking clue. Beta Adam and my dad have been in meetings ever since those rogues stepped on our territory. The she-wolves are gonna love that scar you on your chest," he chuckled with a wink.

I shook my head and glanced down at the pinkish color on my chest as I slid an arm into a sleeve. "Naw, man. Girls don't look at me like that."

He rounded on me, his face in complete shock, "You are blind! Have you not been paying attention? Some of these she-wolves are pressing you hard, and you are oblivious!"

I sighed, running my hand through my hair and down my face, "If they knew me before, they wouldn't want anything to do with me."

The sun rose over the mountains, meaning Sawyer would be late getting to the other wolf waiting on him, and Beta Adam would put him through some crazy shit for his tardiness.

A nurse came into my room and asked if I wanted my breakfast. I nodded, and she brought in the most delicious-looking meal I had seen in a while. Scrambled eggs, sausage links, bacon, pancakes, and skillet potatoes with cheese covered the tray. She also served me O.J. and milk. As she sat it down in front of me, Sawyer seemed to be salivating at the mouth. I thanked her and ravenously dove into the meal.

"Damn, man, they give you the good stuff!"

My eyes were huge as my stomach growled in satisfaction at the pile of food before me, "This is the first non-bland food they've given me."

Sawyer came over and sat on my bed watching me eat. I sighed and handed him one of my sausage links. He took it like he had been starving half his life, and I couldn't help but chuckle. The doctor, Beta, and Alpha came in just as he stuffed the whole thing in his mouth. His eyes were as big as saucers when he spotted the trio in the room. Beta Adam and his father shook their heads and then looked at me. The beta nodded. "You ready, pup?"

I nodded and downed the milk, grabbing a piece of bacon and a pancake. The rest stayed on my plate in the chair. I walked up to them with Sawyer behind me. The Alpha grinned at me, turned, and walked out of the room. We all followed.

Everyone we passed lowered their heads, showing their respect. We made our way out of the hospital building, going to the packhouse. Even though winter surged on, the morning happened to be warm. I figured that we would make our way to the sparing field since I was out of the hospital and today was a sparing day. I couldn't hear anyone down at the arenas as we got closer to the packhouse; the perfume of the many different scents of the wolves seeped out of the cracks.

What's going on?

Sarge tilted his head, his ears forward. *Seems they're having a meeting.*

I rolled my eyes, and Sawyer gave me a questionable look. I just shrugged at him and kept walking.

Note to self—use internal eye roll.

When we entered the packhouse, I understood why the many different scents seeped from the doors. We all went into the dining hall and made our way to the front; I tried to turn down a row and sit down when Beta Adam grabbed my shoulder and pushed me to continue forward. Standing in front of a vast crowd and looking out at them made me nervous. However, Archer was good at this; he could stand in front of whoever and be calm. I could feel the sadness start to take over me, but I sensed Sarge and knew I would be okay. The Beta made me stand beside Sawyer, and they stood in the middle in front of the entire pack.

"As you all know, there was an attack from what we thought were rogues. These wolves were not; they were from another pack. We must keep a good watch on our borders and our pups. As of right now, no pups are to be out without supervision. I urge you all to be diligent and to report any sighting of any strange wolves," the Alpha communicated to his pack. "I want to thank the Beta, my son, and Nolen for fighting off five of the wolves. Killing them all to help protect the pack. You both proved that Beta Adam has trained you well, and each of your packs will be in great hands in the future."

The wolves in the dining room hollered and cheered, others wolf-whistled. Sawyer took it all in stride, but me? I couldn't seem to look them in the face. I glanced over at Beta Adam as he stood there, his arms crossed over his chest.

The Alpha smiled as he looked upon us. I finally looked around and noticed that Amora hid behind her mother's skirts again. She continued to stare at me, those beautiful amber eyes keeping mine. I realized that when she got older, Sawyer and I would be fighting off a ton of males trying to catch her attention. Her scent wafted to me, and my mind became numb to the fantastic odor; her smell had unquestionably gotten more potent, which made me wonder why.

She's a cute pup. A little young, though. Sarge remarked as he pushed his way to the front a little.

Amora is the Alpha's daughter. I told him, a smile playing on my lips.

I see that she is of alpha blood, and she appears to have taken a liking to you, Sarge commented.

Yes, I stood up for her the day after I arrived, I responded.

Sarge laid down, his massive head resting on his front paws. His golden eyes were shining at me.

Yes, I see that now. Like your brother did for you? Sarge inquired, and my heart constricted with his question about my brother.

The pack filed out of the dining hall, and I made my way to my room. I couldn't wait to lay down on my bed. The hospital bed had been soft, but the bed that was mine until my training was done was calling my name. The bad thing was it wasn't even after twelve yet and I was tired. I felt a strong pull to get to bed before I passed out right here in the dining room.

Sleep heals, Sarge remarked to me, his tail wagging.

I bowed my head to the Luna and Amora as I walked past them. They both inclined their heads to me, Amora giving me one of her beautiful grins. When I was halfway up the stairs, I heard a set of footsteps heading my way, and I turned as Beta Adam stopped at the bottom of the stairs. His dark eyes were searching me as he stood there. "I was going to let you know that I'm giving you the rest of the week off. But I expect you to be up and learning from Delta Eric while you are not training with me."

I nodded to him, "Yes, Beta."

"I also wanted to thank you for coming to my rescue that day with Sawyer. If you both hadn't come to help, I would not have been able to see my pup grow up. She was born that morning."

He left me to ponder that information. Beta Adam was now a father; I grinned, turned, and continued up the stairs, into my room, throwing my bag of shredded clothes in the trash and sitting down on my mattress. I was so tired, but my brain was running a mile a minute with everything that had happened since I got here. I could not believe I defeated shifted wolves.

Well, I did help, you know, Sarge huffed as he looked over his shoulder.

I sighed and fell back onto my bed. I was too exhausted to do much else. Laying there, I let my mind wander to Archer, wondering what he would have done in my situation. I wished he were there, then I wouldn't have to be here, and I'd be able to do my own thing.

Archer would be disgusted with my thoughts at the moment. I had to be strong to prove to myself and to the pack I would be running that I could do this. My hand went to the left side of my chest, subconsciously playing with the difference in texture from the blemished skin to the other smooth skin beside it. It unnerved me—another thing I would have to get used to.

CHAPTER FOUR: BIRTHDAY

Today was my birthday. My sixteenth birthday party, to be exact, and Sawyer was being steadfast about holding a party for me. My parents arrived last night, no one else from my pack came, which didn't surprise me. I sat on the side of my bed, listening to the music playing outside and in the dining room.

I'd never had such a big party. After the one when I turned ten and no one showed up my parents had decided to make it a family affair. Friends were scarce with me, which did not bother me, and when I came here, I hadn't expected any type of party here, especially a birthday party.

Believe me, Sawyer had tried the last two times, but I'd told the Luna and the Alpha I didn't want one, which they had humbly accepted. But this time, Sawyer would not let me say no, so I gave up and gave him free rein with it.

To say I dreaded this party would be an understatement; I knew it would be exactly like at my pack, and not having Archer here to help with the blow to my already non-existent self-esteem.

"Nolen?"

I glanced up, and Amora stood near my door. A flattering colorful shirt hung on her torso with a pair of blue jeans that hugged her hips. She'd filled out nicely since I'd arrived here. Her amber eyes stared back at my blue ones; the M shape of her top lip made me want to walk up to her and rub my thumb over it, and across the bottom one as well.

I felt like I was sweating where I sat; my heart drummed in my chest, and if she would have had her wolf, I realized she would have been able to catch it.

Sarge paced the back of my mind as I continued to stare at that beautiful face of hers. I could not understand why she made me feel this way.

"Nolen? Did you hear me?" her sweet voice carried back to me.

"What? Uh, not really. I'm sorry, Amora. Tell me again," I asked her as I stood up, straightening my T-shirt.

"They're waiting on you. Downstairs at your party?" her eyebrow seemed to be flirting with me, along with her grin.

"I know. I... I'm not used to all of this, that's all." She always found a way to make me say more than I wanted when she stared at me with those gorgeous eyes.

"The mighty Alpha heir of Rhyolite pack afraid of a party?" she teased me, her face brightened with the smile that played on her lips.

"No. I'm not used to all this attention."

"Well, get used to it, Nolen, you are going to be Alpha soon, and you are going to be in crowds and other large gatherings." She continued walking around the room I had received when I'd arrived here, fingering my things in the space.

"Well, I guess it will be easier when my Luna is at my side."

"She will be very blessed to have you as a mate. The moon goddess will bless you with a beautiful one, that is for sure." Her eyes danced to the side mischievously as they roamed my form. She picked up one of my books from the shelf. It was a dark book, and there were a few scenes in there that I hoped she wouldn't see.

"I'm afraid she will reject me."

Amora sat the book down and came up to me. The pull to her was a little stronger than before. Her hands lightly touched my arms, and her eyes gazed up at mine through those long black lashes of hers. *Goddess, you made her beautiful*, I thought. Too bad this little minx wouldn't happen to be my mate; I didn't understand if I was falling for her or if this crazy thing with Sarge being with me made things all weird.

Amora gave me one of those mesmerizing looks when she glanced up at me through her lashes, making my breath quicken, and I lost myself in those eyes of hers. "If your mate is stupid enough to reject you, your second chance will prove true love exists, even among werewolves."

"Amora, you realize second chance mates are myths." My hands rested on her hips, her body flushed at my touch and her heart rate increased. I resisted the urge to pull her close to my form, because she was my best friend's sister, and she had just turned thirteen.

"The Goddess would not pair you with someone who would reject you, Nolen." She winked at me and smiled as her rapid heart began to settle back to its normal rhythm.

"She would if she is from my pack."

Amora stepped back from me, admiration in her eyes. "Why, because you think she would be embarrassed? Look at you now, Nolen, all the she-wolves here worship the ground you walk on, along with my brother."

Looking away from her. I stared at one of the other walls, even though I saw her out of the corner of my eye. "You don't understand what they did to me."

She started to respond, her eyes starting to water, when footsteps rang through the hall. I recognized his gait before he came to my door. I stepped away from Amora to a distance to be considered decent. She gave me a hurtful glance until Sawyer walked in, his face full of delight; he came up to me, clapping me on the back as he wrapped his arm around my shoulder. "You need to come on, man. Everyone is waiting on you."

I looked back at Amora, and she gave me a grin before we went out the door.

Amora

After hearing the pain in Nolen's voice about his pack, I believed I needed to do something. But like always, Sawyer was ruining things, and I couldn't help but be sad for Nolen. When I first saw him three years ago, I couldn't help but smile at him.

He used to be such a scrawny boy, but he'd seemed friendly enough. When he had made those boys give me my doll back, I'd been so excited that I had hugged him.

It'd felt right, it truly had, and as we got older, I sensed I needed to be with him, but not like the mate pull, because from what I understood about it, there was no doubt when you experienced the mate pull. Since the rogue attack, his appeal had intensified, but most of the she-wolves were also drawn to him.

I sighed and gazed around his room. He wasn't like most guys with posters of naked girls on his walls. I mean, I had never seen his room at his pack, but from what he'd told me, I didn't think he would put them on his walls at home. I walked out of the room, my hand caressing the book

I laid on his dresser and went back down to the party. I noticed Sawyer had surrounded himself and Nolen with many of the she-wolves, and they hung on their every word.

I shook my head and went to my friends. They weren't as bold as some of the other she-wolves but loved talking about Nolen and Sawyer. I could only handle them talking about Nolen to an extent. Hearing what they wanted to do to my brother grossed me out. I mean, why would you tell someone's sibling what you wanted to do to them?

I walked up to them, smirking at their theatrics over the two alpha heirs at the opposite end of the room. "Hey, girls. Still over here pining for the hot alpha heirs?"

They all giggled, and Anna spoke up, her now purple hair bouncing in her ponytail. I swear the girl had some sort of ADD problem, but she was a good friend. "Girl, you know it! I would love to be one of their mates."

"We all would," Destini professed, pretending to swoon into Sarah's arms. Sarah caught her, and we all giggled out loud, causing a few other wolves to glare at us; my mother shook her head and smiled at me.

I nodded as we continued to stare in my brother and Nolan's direction. Girls were touching him, and one was rubbing up against him; I couldn't deny it made me a little jealous, until he kept backing away from her, and she fell on her ass. I couldn't help but laugh out loud, which caught her attention.

Nolen tried to help her from the ground, but she slapped his hand away and got up. Her face was red with anger and embarrassment as she stalked toward me and got in my face, growling; I never wavered as I looked her in the eyes. "What are you laughing about?"

Shrugging at her question, I gave her a little bit of sass that my brother Sawyer always told me to keep at a minimum. There was no way I was going to let this female come at me and try to dominate me. I'm of Alpha blood—that shit was not going to fly with me anymore. "You, I mean, you keep putting yourself onto him, and he keeps trying to move away from you. So, it would be best if you learned when to stop."

I spotted my brother and Nolen making their way up to me. The weak little girl when Nolen first came here no longer existed. Nolen was the reason I'd decided I wouldn't be the girl who got trampled on. He had shown me that there was no time like now to make changes. I'd finally talked Dad into letting me train with the warriors, and oh how I excelled in it. I even took down wolves a little older than me, so she didn't scare me.

"You mouthy little brat! You don't know if he likes it or not!"

I started to say something back to her when Nolen came up beside me, and Sawyer stood on the other side. Their auras radiating off them, causing the lower ranked wolves to cower. But not me. I wouldn't let them do that to me. My brother's alpha voice sounded out beside me, trying to get me to submit. "Is there a problem, ladies?"

I could not for the life of me say anything with Nolen being so close to me. He gave off this crazy amount of power, and it caused goosebumps to run down my body. I took a chance to gaze up at him, catching him glancing at me. I swore that I spotted his eye color flicker from his dark blue. I gazed back to the she-wolf who was in front of me, her hard eyes on mine. "I have no problem with this bitch."

The she-wolf in question snarled and started to come forward when a deep growl to my left gave her pause. She glanced over to Nolen and then back at me. She huffed, turned on her heel, and stormed out of the room. I heard Sawyer sigh beside me, and I turned to him with a glare; they both always did this. They always came to my aid when I didn't need them to. Always treating me like a little girl!

Sawyer ran his hand down his face before gazing down at me. I always seemed to get under his skin, but this would have been fine if I was a boy. "Amora, you are going to have to stop doing that."

"I didn't start anything. It wasn't my fault she decided to land on her ass. I would have been able to take her; you both didn't need to come to my rescue," I replied, glancing between my brother and Nolen. My gaze lingered on Nolen a little longer than I intended because that feeling swept through me again. I was so confused, but this wolf seemed to exist to make me feel things that I didn't think I should allow myself to feel. My heart started to race, and his head cocked to the side as if he heard it in my chest. Goddess, why did you make this wolf so damn gorgeous!

Nolen's parents came up to him then, and I realized he had grown taller since he came to my pack. He was now almost as tall as his father, and they nearly passed for twins, if not for his father's grey hair. I bowed my head in respect to them, and his mother smiled. Without a doubt, he had his mother's demeanor, and I hoped he would continue to keep it when he took over. These packs didn't need another tyrant to run them. Though Nolen's father wasn't a tyrant, he was still a little more forceful than Nolen.

"It's about time to eat cake. Are you ready, Nolen?" she asked him. Her voice was like the swift but gentle water in the creek.

He turned to his mother and father and nodded. He glanced back to me but walked off with them and my brother. I watched them meet up with my parents and realized he would be leaving for his pack in a year and a half to finish his training with his father.

I would never see him again unless in passing, and even that would be rare. He would become Alpha, and when he shifted for the first time, he would find his mate. The tears bubbled up in my eyes and I fought them back.

I would not cry, he was a good friend, and I was glad I had been able to meet him. The thought of losing that friend made me sad, but his destiny would win over my feelings. Would it be too much to ask to be his? To be able to stay with him for the rest of my life? Was it wrong I considered asking him to be my chosen mate? It would be selfish of me, right? *Moon Goddess, please guide me down the right path.*

I walked up to the group standing between my brother and Nolen as he blew out his birthday candles, a contagious smile on his lips. His smile always warmed my heart, making me smile with him, and when he glanced over to me, my cheeks burned, turning my skin red.

CHAPTER FIVE: CHALLENGE

NOLEN

I continued my training with the Beta and the Delta, trying to soak in everything they taught me. They told me I learned quicker than most trainees, and no wolf would be able to stand in my way once fully shifted.

I had not told them about Sarge coming to me early. He had been insistent that no one should know but me and that he would be concealed by the Goddess herself. No, I hadn't been able to shift yet, but he existed there in my head, giving me pointers and helping me put the older wolves who decided to spar with Sawyer and me on their asses.

On the days we had to ourselves, I spent them resting and reading books in my room. I would sometimes hang out with Sawyer and other times Amora. But things were getting weird when I spent time near her.

I couldn't help but be protective of her, and I chalked it up to the time I stood up for her. Just like Archer used to stand up for me. The intense need to protect her filled me, not because she happened to be a good friend of mine but also because she was my best friend's sister, which made her like my sister.

Whenever she was around, this pull to her became more intense. Like how a moth flew to a flame. When I left before my eighteenth birthday, I discerned that I would probably never see her again, and when she turned eighteen and shifted, she would find her mate.

Someone who would take care of her, would give her strong pups and make her happy, because if he didn't, I would make sure he never hurt her again. She always talked about saving all her firsts for her mate, which made me wonder if mine had the same ideals.

I mean, hell, I was still a virgin, not that she-wolves didn't want me now. That's all they wanted to do was take me to bed with them. But not Amora; she still treated me like she always did. Though I had caught her staring at me a few times, which boosted my self-confidence. Smiling to myself, I shook my head and tried to return to my studies.

She is very pretty, Nolen. You shouldn't worry about things like this right now. When we shift, we will see, Sarge commented as he seemed to lay down inside my head.

I understand, Sarge, but it's just weird with her right now. I sense this pull to her, and I don't think I should. The urge to be right beside her all the time is becoming more intense each day, I reasoned with him. He just lay there, his ears at attention. I sighed. I could never find out anything from him about Amora and these crazy-ass feelings I had. I glanced up and realized that the Delta was standing above me, his arms crossed over his chest.

I panicked and started to fumble with my papers and my book on my desk, glancing up to the board to see if I might be able to pick up on what question he had asked me during my daydream. After a few seconds, I gave up and looked back up at him. "Sorry, sir, can you repeat the question?"

"Nolen, I have been trying to get your attention for the past ten minutes. What is going on in that head of yours?" His facial features were full of concern as we stared at each other. Then he shook his head, covering his face with his hand.

"I'm sorry, sir. It won't happen again." He removed his hand and gave me a questioning look as he strolled back up to the front of the small room. Sawyer silently laughed at me. Balling up a piece of paper, I sent it flying toward Sawyer, hitting him square in the head. He turned on me, giving me a glare and a mischievous grin. I shook my head and made myself concentrate on what the Delta was doing in front of me. I had a few more hours before we were released out of this office for the rest of the afternoon to ourselves.

"Nolen, what would you do if an enemy pack released smaller portions of their warriors to come from the east and west but a more significant amount of them came from the south?"

Looking him in the eyes, I sat up straighter. Confident in what I would do in this scenario. "I would send my best warriors to the south and two smaller groups to the east and the west with another group protecting the older wolves, pregnant wolves, and pups."

"That's good reasoning, but what if there happened to be a surprise group coming from the north?" Delta Eric crossed his arms as he stood at the front of the room.

I pondered the question before answering him; Sawyer stared at me, waiting for my answer. I couldn't think of anything else but a last-ditch effort to protect my pack. "I would challenge the Alpha to a dual to protect my pack from harm."

"The thing about this scenario, Nolen, is that there isn't a pretty picture to keep everyone safe. Challenging the Alpha is a bold choice, but it might also be the death of more of your pack if you are defeated. You have to understand not all Alphas give mercy to defeated packs. You have to make sure you can protect your pack. As an Alpha, you are going to make choices that will mean death to some of the pack. Unfortunately, it's what happens, and the warriors understand that could be their fate." The Delta stood at the front staring at me. His green eyes locked on me as he waited for me to answer him.

"But that is not acceptable. I should be just as willing to lay down my life for my pack as they are for me," I countered, my brows furrowed in confusion. Why would I expect my pack to die for me if I wasn't willing to do the same?

Spoken like a true Alpha! Sarge commented, a surge of pride filling me.

I couldn't tell if the Delta's facial expression held admiration or sadness; the slight smile on his face and his body language confused me. He turned away from me and started to write on the board. I looked over at Sawyer, he was grinning up a storm and gave me a thumbs up.

Once we were finished with the battle tactics, we went out and made our way over to the game room in the packhouse to let off some steam. We started with some pool, then played some video games. More of the guys came in, and we took turns in playing against each other.

"Hey, Nolen, how bout we arrange a sparring match. See who is actually the strongest out of us." Bringing my attention to Vorn as he leaned up against the wall, surveying the other players. He had recently turned eighteen and shifted, so he had his wolf to help him, which truthfully didn't worry me. He was still strong, though, and I would have to keep in mind what he could do.

I'm with you too, Sarge told me as he eyed the other male through mine.

I know, buddy, but he doesn't realize I have you. I laughed internally at my crazy wolf. Sarge snorted, and I turned to Sawyer, who shrugged. Glancing back to Vorn, I met his gaze with determination. "Okay, when?"

"How about tonight? Round up all the pack to come to see you get your ass handed to you." He roared with laughter; his dark brown eyes gleamed mercilessly. The wolves around him glanced between him and me.

"Okay, Vorn, but I doubt I'll be getting my ass handed to me." Everyone in the room watched in wonder. Vorn had started to make a name for himself since he got his wolf. He was ruthless and possibly one of the strongest warriors in training. But he still had a lot to learn about a fight. I had observed him and the older wolves he fought with and realized how to defeat him. I stood up and walked over to him. Towering slightly over him, as I'd grown into my own. I couldn't believe the confidence that seeped through me. It felt good. "I'll meet you on the sparring field. You better hope you can keep up."

Vorn snorted in my face, and Sarge tried to surge forward, but I would not let another wolf realize his presence right now. I walked away to go to the Beta, letting him know that I had a challenge from another wolf. When I got to his office, I caught the scent of the Alpha and the Delta in the small room and knocked on the door, waiting for him to invite me in.

"Come in."

I opened the door, walked in, and closed the door behind me. They all three glanced up at me as I stood in the office waiting to be granted permission to speak.

"What can I do for you, Nolen?" The Beta stared at me, giving me a questioning glance. He seemed to know why I had come.

"I came to tell you that Vorn challenged me. He wants to spar tonight, sir," I responded, holding my head high as I gazed over them behind the desk.

He glanced at me and then strolled around his desk that he stood behind with the Alpha. The other two wolves in the room stared at me. "And you accepted?"

"Yes, sir."

"You realize he has his wolf, and this is not a two on one match." His eyes brightened, and he threw a grin my way. His hand took hold of his jaw as he waited for my answer.

"I can handle him, sir," I told him, puffing myself up. Determination pushed through my aura, and Sarge came forward a bit.

The Beta walked back over to the Alpha behind his desk, "Okay, well, we will arrange everything. Be sure you eat enough to give you energy but not enough to make you sick."

I nodded and walked back out of the office to my room to relax before the match. I sat on my bed staring at the room I had been using for the last three years; I had one more year here, and then my dad would be drilling the rest of my alpha training into me. Making me an alpha that he could be proud of.

No need to be nervous, Nolen, Sarge told me. I grinned; he was getting better at knowing my emotions. Hell, I was getting better at reading his. This is why we would be victorious. Once we shifted, we would be even more connected.

I know; I'm just nervous that they will find out that I've possessed your strength since the rogue attack. I hadn't even told Sawyer, and if he found out, I didn't know if he would be mad at me for keeping it from him. There was no way I could afford to lose the only real friend I had here.

So what? We are one and the same. Just like Vorn and his wolf.

Sarge was right, we were one, but would they see that since I shouldn't have any part of him till I was eighteen?

I understand that; I'm glad that I have you now. I don't think I would have gotten through all of this after Archer passed. In fact, I knew it would've been much more brutal; ever since Sarge had appeared, I'd been a little more whole than before.

Sarge whimpered; his ears drooped slightly before he perked them back up. *You realize you did all this yourself, and I only helped a little in the sparring matches.*

Really?

Yes, I only helped when absolutely needed. Like when you needed me when those wolves attacked.

I heard the knock on my door and saw Sawyer in the doorway. My best friend grinned at me as he leaned against my doorframe, his arms tightly crossed. "You ready to get something to eat?"

I got up from my bed, stretched, and walked up to him. We were about the same height now, but I was a little taller than him. "Yeah, I need to make sure I put that wolf in his place."

Sawyer laughed with me as we made our way down to get something to eat. Everyone kept watching me; I realized they thought I was way over my head. But I would show them just what I could do, and putting Vorn on his ass happened to be my goal, whether it be in his human form or his wolf.

When we got to the dining hall, Amora and her friends were already there at their usual table, eating and whispering together. Every once in a while, I could make out what they were saying but not enough to figure out what they were talking about.

I sat down with Sawyer, and an omega brought us some food. I only ate the meat and some carbs, but I made sure I didn't stuff myself. Vorn sat in the corner, not even eating anything, but he was weird like that. It looked like he was meditating, leaning up against the wall, his eyes closed.

The Alpha and the Beta came in, and everyone got quiet, waiting on the news of whether the challenge would continue. Because, ultimately, it happened to be Beta Adam's decision to let it happen, and because I didn't have my wolf in their eyes, they could keep the challenge from going forward. Which I hoped they didn't because this would be the only way for me to show Vorn I could take him down without Sawyer.

The Alpha gazed over the crowd in the dining room and then looked at Vorn and me, giving us both a stern gaze. "I want to let you all know a challenge has been issued. Vorn has challenged Nolen for his place in the sparring ranks. We will be holding this match tonight at the sparring fields. As the challengers are eating, we will be getting everything ready for the challenge. When the individuals in the challenge are done eating, they will make their way to the sparring fields."

I nodded to the Alpha and the Beta. I glanced back over to Vorn, who had gotten up and started to make his way out of the dining room. As he walked past me, my heart rate increased; I wasn't nervous about the fight with him. No, it was the possibility that everyone would recognize I had Sarge.

Amora and her friends had gotten up from their table, and I looked over at Sawyer as he sat in front of me at our table. I motioned for him to follow me, not confident I could speak at the moment. There was no way I could eat another bite. Sawyer nodded, got up, and we made our way out of the packhouse.

CHAPTER SIX: NEW SCARS AND TATS

S awyer and I made our way down to the sparring fields. Vorn strutted in front of us while the Alpha and Beta Adam led the group. Sawyer kept glancing at me from his peripherals as we ambled down to where the challenge would take place.

"So you sure you want to go through with this? I mean, he does have his wolf after all, and you, well, don't."

"Yes, I am sure. I'm not afraid of him or his wolf. We fought rogues at thirteen in wolf form; I can handle this wolf," I told him. More confidence radiated from me than I felt. He seemed to believe me this time around and decided to let me be. We continued to the field, the rest of the pack following us. Amora's tempting scent floated from behind me, and I tried my best to keep from turning to glance at her. Which didn't work because I caught myself glancing back at her one more time, even after I told myself it would be the last.

When we got to the fields, the lights shined brightly against the darkening sky. The moon was full tonight, so it would help strengthen both of us. Vorn thought it would give him the advantage. This could also be why he wanted to spar now and not another day. He wanted the full moon's help. Could he be afraid of me?

Both Vorn and I stepped into the middle of the field; he had stripped to a pair of basketball shorts. I knew then he planned on shifting to be able to bring me down. I smirked at him, and he scowled at me. I pulled off my T-shirt, throwing it to the ground.

My muscles rippled under my skin as I stretched my arms. Gasps came from the rest of the pack in the stands, and it resonated in my ears as my scar showed bright against my tanned skin. I had made sure to keep a shirt on at all times. I didn't want people to see them, as I was still getting used to them, even though they were more than three years old.

Vorn's eyes went to the claw marks on my chest, then back to my eyes. He didn't show any hesitation or willingness to leave, even now. I wasn't going to leave until I defeated him or he beat me; he would not gain the satisfaction of my forfeiting the match. We turned to the Alpha's box, where the Alpha and Beta Adam sat with their mates. Beta Adam glanced between the both of us, making sure we were listening to him. "This will be a fight to submission; you can use either form. There will be no life-threatening wounds, and if there are, you will be disqualified. You may begin when you are ready."

"You won't be so high and mighty when I'm finished with you," Vorn declared as he shifted into a massive reddish-brown wolf. He snarled at me, saliva dripping off his fangs as his jowls pulled up away from his teeth, revealing dagger-sharp fangs, his growl ripping from his throat. I took a fighting stance and waited for him to make the first move.

I needed to be able to see if he was still doing the same old thing or if he had decided to take the more senior wolves' advice. Vorn rushed me, and I jumped to the side, slapping him on the backside just above his tail like I would if punishing a dog. He turned, snapping and snarling at me, his eyes ablaze with fury now.

I think you pissed him off, Sarge laughed in my mind; his tongue lolled to the side of his mouth. He was already enjoying this, and it had just gotten started.

I think so too. But this is just strategy, I informed him while I kept my eyes on his movements. He was a sneaky bastard, and one wrong move from me could mean defeat.

He charged me again his overconfidence showing in his eyes; I juked him but his teeth sliced through my right forearm. Blood poured down my arm and onto the ground. Vorn rushed me again and collided with me with his shoulder, throwing me through the air, my back hitting the ground, knocking the breath from my lungs. The small pebbles in the grass dug into my skin as I slid to a stop. Those pebbles stung, but now was not the time to worry about that.

Boos rang out from the crowd after the hit. Vorn's wolf stalked to me as I got up from the earth; I surveyed him as he circled me, snarling and snapping at my legs, trying to make me jump, I stayed calm while he continued to revolve around me.

I gazed up at the full moon in the black sky; its silvery rays shone down upon us. I heard him lunge, and I slowed my breathing and turned, twisting away from him just in time. Taking hold of his extended back leg, I threw him across the field; he landed with a thud but sprang to his feet.

He looked like a rabid animal, foam coming from his mouth, and charged at me. I heard the sharp intake of breath from the crowd, knowing this would be the end for me. I crouched low to be able to do what I needed to go under his colossal head. He jumped, his front legs extended, and his toes on his paws stretched out, ready to dig his claws into whatever part of me he could.

When he got over me, I rose up and grabbed the massive wolf around the neck. The force of his lunge and me coming in contact with him threw us both to the ground. I tightened my hold on him, trying to put him to sleep.

Vorn kept struggling to free himself until he finally passed out. I placed his head on the ground, and he shifted back to his human form. I turned to face the Beta and the Alpha, bowing my head; they each bowed theirs to me—my chest heaving from the exertion of the match. I grabbed my forearm to apply pressure to it to stop the bleeding, the high of the adrenaline fading and the wounds hurting more than before.

"Victory goes to Nolen!" The Alpha shouted, a beaming smile on his face. Beta Adam was pleased as well; I mean, he should've been—he had been my instructor since I got here.

The crowd erupted into a roar as they rose to their feet, jumping and stomping. I glanced around and noticed Amora gazing down at me. Sarge's emotions raged with mine after our battle with Vorn. I felt my eyes flicker, and I knew she saw it because her face turned to shock. I turned from her, picked up my shirt, and walked off the sparring field.

)))) 🐺 (((((

Sawyer caught up with me after almost making it back to the packhouse. I had my shirt over my arm, keeping the blood from trailing behind me. The minor cuts on my back tingled as they healed; the one on my arm was extremely painful after all the adrenaline subsided. Sarge lay curled up in the back of my mind. Sawyer clapped me on the shoulder, bringing my attention to him. "Hey, man, are you not going to go to the doc?"

"No, it's clotting now," I told him as I walked up to my room. He continued to follow me, and I realized he wanted to ask me something. I walked into my bathroom, threw my shirt in the dirty laundry basket, and turned on the faucet at the sink to run warm water over the wound. It wasn't deep enough for stitches, but I needed to use some steri-strips to hold it together until it healed, or should I say Sarge healed the gaping wound. Sawyer continued to lean up against the doorway, waiting for me to elaborate on what I had said.

"I think you need to let me in on your little secret, man. There is no way that you could've done what you did without a wolf." He didn't sound pissed, but he could very well be. Sawyer had a knack for controlling his emotions.

I glanced up at him through the mirror and sighed; I pulled a rag from the rack and put pressure on the wound again, leaning up against the sink counter as I inspected him, trying to gauge his emotions. "It's because I already have him. I just can't shift till I turn eighteen."

"You mean you could have beat my ass this entire time but you chose not to?" Sawyer's mouth opened wide in shock as he eyed me. He didn't look pissed, but like I said, he was good at holding in his emotions.

"No, Sarge only helps if I need him to."

"So, can you find your mate now?"

"No, unless she is not in this pack. But no, I don't know who she is yet."

Sawyer pondered something as we both stood there in my bathroom. The tingling on my back faded and started again on my arm. It was so weird that I could heal like this now, but it would still scar since I didn't fully have my wolf. "What is it like to have him in your head?"

"I don't know; I mean, at first it was weird because I could only hear him. But as time went on, I could start to see some of him." Shrugging my shoulders, I glanced over at him, wondering if he remembered when I outwardly rolled my eyes.

"How long have you had him?" I could tell the wheels in his mind were running over the last few years we had been friends, if I had changed and if there were clues that he had missed.

"Since the rogue attack."

"Why did you not tell me? I thought we were friends?"

"We are, Sawyer, but at that time, I didn't really understand what was happening. I was kind of nervous about the whole thing. Plus, I had only been here for a couple of months and didn't know how much I could tell anyone." I felt shitty at that moment for not telling him, but how do you start that conversation?

"It's cool, man. I mean, I will be shifting in a year. What's cool is you will still be here when I do, and you can give me pointers." He chuckled as he pushed off the doorframe.

"Yeah. That will be cool. But then after that I have to leave. It'll be kind of weird when I go back to my pack." There was no doubt that it would be weird. They all hated me and didn't want me to be their alpha. We stood there for a moment, letting the silence take over. I took the rag off my arm, and a small scar where the wound had been had developed.

Sawyer's eyes went to the scar on my chest before coming back to meet mine. He had that mischievous grin on his face like he was fixing to suggest some crazy off-the-wall adventure. "Why don't we go get some tats."

"We can't, we aren't old enough yet." I had always wanted to get a tattoo, but I didn't know of anyone that would do tats since for most human shops, you had to be eighteen and provide proof you were. Otherwise, they would turn you away.

Sawyer shrugged as he crossed his arms, the grin still plastered on his face. "I know one of the artists, plus he's a werewolf. So he'll be willing to tat us up."

I thought about it and then nodded. What was it going to hurt? I mean, now was the perfect opportunity. "Okay, when?"

"How about this weekend?"

"Beta Adam is gonna have our heads." I laughed and Sawyer laughed with me. I followed him to the doorway of my room. It was late, and we both had to be up to run early in the morning. Just as Sawyer left to go to his room, Amora emerged at the top of the stairs, talking and laughing with her friends.

I couldn't believe how gorgeous she'd gotten in the three years I'd lived here. She spotted me staring at her, and I glimpsed a blush forming on her cheeks. Amora's eyes shifted to the scar on my chest before she brought them back up to mine. There had been times when her hand had brushed across it, and I wondered if it disgusted her.

Her friends continued to talk around her as we stared at each other. If I were destined to have my mate reject me, like I realized I would be, I could only dream to convince Amora to be my chosen mate. But then, I didn't want her to miss out on the love she was fated for. She deserved all the nice things the Moon Goddess gave her. If she were fated to an alpha, she would make an excellent Luna, and if she weren't, she would be amazing at whatever she was destined to be.

I winked at her, and she gave me a little grin as she passed by my room. I couldn't believe the confidence I had to make me do that. I closed my door, took the rest of my clothes off, and jumped in the shower. Afterward, I crashed on my bed, falling asleep instantly.

That was the first night I dreamed of Amora; her beautiful eyes tortured me in my sleep. I wanted to be able to stay in that dream with her and never leave.

CHAPTER SEVEN: TATTOOS

The rest of the week went by faster than I thought it would. After the fight with Vorn, everyone wanted to find out how I did it, and I kept that secret to myself, as did Sawyer. The girls didn't care how I did it but were even more nagging about wanting to be with me. So there I was, holed up in my room, trying to keep away from the un-mated females.

I sat on my bed, waiting for Sawyer to finish getting ready so we could go. We had to let Sawyer's dad know that we would be leaving the territory since I was not from the pack and just a guest. Beta Adam still didn't grasp where our adventure happened to be taking us. Luckily, the wolf who would be doing the tats was from another pack. Leaning back on the bed, my hand clasped behind my head, I closed my eyes, about ready to say fuck it and not go.

That's when my door burst open and slammed shut. I swiftly sat up, ready for anything that had come into my room. Amora stood there, her back to my door, laughing, as whoever was on the other side of it banged on the wooden structure. Tilting my head, I raised one of my eyebrows at her. "What did you do this time?"

She grinned at me as she approached, her eyes gleaming with playfulness. The only thing I could think she had done was piss another wolf off. "Well, I could've intentionally poured cold water over one of the younger warriors."

I shook my head as the banging continued on my door; it seemed this wolf did not realize this happened to not be her room but mine. I got up, walked past her, and jerked the door open. He was about to swing his fist again when he realized the door was no longer closed, and I stood there in the doorway. When he saw me, he stumbled backward, stammering. "Sorry, Nolen, I thought this was Amora's room. I didn't know she ran into yours."

"Get out of here; you're getting the fucking floors wet. I'd hate for someone to actually do something to you other than pour water on you." Sarge's alpha voice seeping through into mine. I had never wanted to use this with any other wolf, but he had pissed me off by banging on my door. He had his wolf; he could have used his nose to realize that it wasn't her room but mine.

The male ran off back down the stairs, slipping in a few of the wet spots. Amora laughed hysterically behind me, and as I turned saw she was doubled over on my bed. She continued to laugh as she gasped for breath. "Oh, My Goddess! That was hilarious! He was soo fucking scared!"

"Amora, these pranks are going to get you into trouble one day." She splayed out on my bed, her arms above her head, grabbing hold of my pillow and laying her head on it. Amora grinned at me, a little of the skin on her stomach showing. I faintly heard a door shut, but her captivating eyes held mine at that moment, and I had completely forgotten I was waiting on Sawyer to come out of his room.

The footsteps in the hall brought me back to reality, especially when I got a whiff of Sawyer making his way to my room. My heart raced as I pulled my gaze from hers and glanced over my shoulder to see how far away he was. Turning my eye on her again, I motioned for her to sit up as I quietly shut the door. "You need to sit up. Your brother is almost to my room, and if he sees you like that on my bed, he will flip his shit."

Amora seemed to have been in the same stupor as I was in moments before. She scampered to a sitting position as Sawyer made it to my room, and I figured he would still probably question why she was sitting on my bed. The knock on my door let me know he was there, my heart raced faster in my chest, and I figured he would be able to hear it even without his wolf.

"Hey, man, you ready to go? We have to be there in about an hour."

I turned and walked up to him, placing a hand on his shoulder, trying to keep his eyes from his sister in my room. "Yep. I've been ready, prima donna."

Amora got up, and that's when he gave me one of those looks he gave the other unmated males in the pack before glancing back to his sister. Confusion sat on his face as he tried to put two and two together. "Why are you in Nolen's room?"

"Because I pulled a prank on Frankie, and he chased me up here. Instead of going to my room, which was further down the hall, I ran in here because

I knew brother Nolen would protect me." Her head swung back and forth with one of her eyebrows cocked, her hands planted on her hips. I breathed an internal sigh of relief, even though nothing had been going on with us other than that moment our eyes had connected.

Sawyer rolled his eyes and walked away, I glanced back at her, and she gave me a wink. I chuckled and walked out of my room, following Sawyer down the stairs. Some of the pack were now up and going about their business. They all bowed their heads as we passed them; we walked out and got into one of the cars sitting in the front.

In all the years I had been here, I had never been off the pack grounds. We pulled through the modest little town beside the territory. The trees that lined the one-lane street were giant compared to the newer cities that we had passed. The buildings appeared as if they had been here for centuries. Sawyer pulled up to a small, newer building, neon signs in the window. He killed the engine, and we got out of the car. As we walked up to the front door, I spotted a few older guys sitting on a patio playing chess. Sarge paced in my mind, and I couldn't figure out why.

We walked in, and a petite she-wolf behind the counter glanced up. Her face brightened when she spotted us; Sawyer walked up with a smile and gave her a wink. The smell inside the establishment floated over to me; leather and rain evaporated from a diffuser somewhere.

She blushed as she stood up to walk out from behind her workspace, her chocolate brown eyes roaming Sawyer and then myself. "So, you two must be the ones wanting a tattoo. Brandon is in the back. I'll go find him for you."

We both nodded to her, and she strolled to the back of the building. Sawyer and I started to look around at all the artwork on the walls. I was looking at one that showed a moon and two wolves howling at it when they came back through the door. He cleared his throat, bringing my full attention to him. "So, what are you thinking on getting and where?"

I turned to him; his dark brown eyes never wavered from mine. The she-wolf who had gone to find him sat back down behind the counter, working on something in front of her. He was my height, if not a little taller; I pulled off my shirt to show him where I wanted the tattoo. "I want something that can cover this and another one to cover this one on my forearm."

He examined both spots before he motioned for Sawyer and me to follow him. We all walked to the back to where a chair and a stool sat. He had all types of inks lining his shelves and ink guns on the counter.

Brandon opened drawers pulling out unopened needles; he glanced over his shoulder, nodding his head to the chair.

I walked over to the chair as Sawyer stood behind me. Brandon sat down on the stool, pulled a metal tray over to us, and placed inks and the unopened packages on the metal surface. "So, I was working on this idea for a big piece, but no one needed something like it. Would you be interested? It has a couple of wolves in front of a new moon with a compass in the moon; what do you think?"

I thought it over a moment before Sarge pushed an image into my mind. I liked his idea and decided to see what Brandon thought. "What about the new moon and compass but with a head of a wolf shaded like a yin and yang symbol."

"I like your imagination." Nodding, he got to work. I had shaved whatever hair that grew on my chest the night before so he wouldn't have to dry shave me. I laid my head back and felt the needle pierce my skin; it didn't hurt as bad as I had thought it would. He drew the image freehand with the tattoo gun.

A few hours later, Brandon had the image permanently on my chest; the scar beneath it was hardly visible. I could not have been happier with the portrait he had etched into my skin. I peeked down at the wings running up my forearm; the blue eyes of a wolf were the first thing I saw. I was proud of both tattoos that Brandon had placed on me. Especially the one drawn for Archer.

Sawyer sat in the chair now, getting Goddess knows what. I continued to gaze at the perfect artwork on my body, and I wondered what Amora would think about them. I chuckled; she always seemed to come into my mind at the most random times.

"What are you over there laughing about?" Sawyer walked up behind me; his new tattoo ran across his chest. The wolf's entire body stretched across his pecks as a ghost of a human ran with him. The ever-changing moon curved above them.

Turning to him, I shook my head. I didn't want him to know that his sister had been on my mind since that morning. He would probably kill me, best friend or not; she was still his little sister. Brandon was cleaning up his workstation, the smell of ink and blood in the room was quickly being removed with disinfectant.

Brandon wrapped the new ink with plastic wrap, and we both walked back upfront with him. Sawyer pulled out his credit card and paid for the work, and I pulled my shirt back on as we got back into the car. The old men were gone from the other patio when we left, which was not abnormal since we had been in the building for quite some time.

Sawyer will be hurting come training day, Sarge told me with a laugh, his tail beating against the ground. If he was ever in a room, that tail would definitely cause some damage.

He won't show it, though, I answered, glancing back over to Sawyer as he drove without his shirt on. He was clearly proud of the tattoo, because the smile on his face never left the whole trip back.

We pulled onto the territory as the sun was setting, and Sawyer pulled the car back where it had previously been parked. We got out, and Sawyer shot me a grin over the vehicle's roof. "What do you think dad and the Beta are going say?"

"I don't know, Sawyer, but I do know that if anyone spots that on you before you tell your dad, he will be pissed." I nodded, glancing over at his shirtless chest. He nodded back and reached into the car, pulling out his shirt and hurriedly throwing it on. We continued into the packhouse; the smell of food filled the first floor. My stomach growled, making me realize I hadn't eaten all day. I steered Sawyer into the dining room just as Danika and her group of friends were going in. She turned around and smacked Sawyer in the chest. "So, where have you two been? Having a day to yourselves?"

Sawyer grimaced, bringing his hand to the fresh tattoo on his chest, smiling at Danika. He winked at her, trying to hide the pain from the playful slap. "We've been out exploring and making new friends."

She gave him a suspicious look before she flipped her ponytail in his face and walked away. Her friends followed her into the dining room. Nudging him forward, we entered the room and sat down at a table. We waited for one of the omegas to bring us a plate of the delicious food cooked by the kitchen staff. He repeatedly glanced over his shoulder at the group of girls Danika was sitting with. I shook my head, chuckling at him. "She's got you pretty good, man. You might want to tell your dad fairly quick; otherwise, something is going to happen to that tat."

A couple of omegas brought a tray and started to sit down plates of food. Along with rolls and butter, they left drinks on the table as well. Mumbling thank yous, we both dug into the food like the wolves we were. I don't think I even chewed it as I shoveled the food in my mouth.

While my mouth was full, Amora sat down beside me with a smile. Her sweet aroma overpowered the scent of the food. I was glad my mouth was stuffed, since it muffled the sigh. "So, y'all were gone for a while. What were you doing? Cause dad has been looking for you both."

Swallowing the mixture of carbs and meat, Sawyer glanced up from his almost finished plate of food, staring at her. "Yeah, and what was he looking for us for?"

"Well, I'm quite sure he got wind of you both going into town to get inked." She glanced at the one on my forearm before flicking them back to my eyes. The pupils had dilated as she stared at me; I turned my gaze from hers as I swallowed the bolus of food.

Sawyer and I both shared a worried glance. Someone must have spotted us at the tat shop; there was no other way. My thoughts went back to the old men playing chess on the patio over the other building. None of them had smelled like a wolf, but Sarge was pacing in my head the entire time. "So, he figured it out?"

"Yep." She popped her lips as she crossed her arms on the table, glancing between the both of us.

Sawyer stared at Amora, fury across his face. He leaned over the table to her, his face in hers. "Damn it. Did you tell him?"

"No! Why would I tell on y'all?"

Sawyer swept his gaze around the room; I assumed to look for his dad. I also scanned the room but didn't see him at his table. That's when I spotted one of the older men who had been playing chess that morning, sitting talking with a few of the younger pups, and it clicked. He was the one who'd told. "Sawyer, I'm sure it wasn't Amora that told him."

Sawyer rounded his eyes on me as he held my gaze, neither one of us budging. "What do you mean? She was the only one that could have."

"No, the old man at the table with the pups? He was playing chess with a few other older men on the patio of that restaurant beside the tat shop." I nodded my head in his direction to make Sawyer look. Both Amora and Sawyer turned toward him; I watched out of the corner of my eye as he glanced up, smiled, and then waved at Sawyer. Sawyer waved back, and then I smelled the Beta and the Alpha as they entered the room along with the Luna. Sawyer confirmed I was correct when his eyes became huge. Sitting my drink down, I braced myself for what came next.

The large hands of the Beta landed heavily on my shoulders, and I flinched before he decided to put more pressure on the freshly tatted skin. I gritted my teeth as he flexed his fingers into my shoulders. "So, boys, did you have fun today?"

Sawyer glanced behind me as I sat there waiting for him to say something. Urging him with my eyes since Beta Adam's grip kept tightening. "Dad, Beta. Nolen and I thought we would get some tattoos. Nolen has been somewhat down about the scars on his chest, so I thought getting it covered up would help."

"Well, what's done is done. Just remember that training doesn't stop because you two are hurting, right, Beta?" Sawyer's dad spoke up behind me. If my hearing was right, laughter was in his tone. That could be a good thing or a bad thing; I just didn't know which at the moment.

"That's right, Alpha. Too bad the coming weeks will be more strenuous than before." Slapping my left shoulder twice, he and the Alpha strolled up to their table, their guffaws of laughter ringing throughout the dining room.

Sarge had curled up in the back of my mind, and I could have sworn that he laughed at me. The prick would have his day. I won't forget this, that was for sure. Amora got up from the table and ran her hand over my shoulder blades. I swear, sometimes I thought that girl wanted more than she was letting on.

CHAPTER EIGHT: FUTURE ALPHA AND LUNA

AMORA

The past several months had been torture. Losing one of my best friends depressed me; I tried to spend as much time as possible with him without seeming weird. But Beta Adam had been keeping them out longer, trying to get them ready to take over their respective packs.

Today, I had been asked to watch the Beta female's little girl, Rachel, and we were playing in the backyard when Sawyer, Beta Adam, and Nolen walked out of the woods. The little pup squealed when she spotted her daddy and sprinted to him. She was the spitting image of him. I felt sorry for the beta female; Rachel was utterly a daddy's girl.

I grinned when the massive man smiled and threw her in the air, catching her on the way down. The little girl giggled, wrapped her arms around her dad's neck, and pecked him on the cheek. Glancing around, I spotted Nolen, and the way he stared at me sent goosebumps down my arms. The tattoo he had stood out, his bare chest glistening with sweat in the setting sun.

My breath caught in my chest as he walked past me, and I couldn't help but shiver at his closeness. I stalked him with my eyes as he and Sawyer went into the packhouse. Turning, I noticed that Beta Adam was still watching me, and Rachel was giggling behind her hand. I reached out for the little girl, trying to divert his attention away from that encounter. "If you want, Beta Adam, I can continue to play with her here in the yard."

Chuckling, he shook his head as he walked past me. "Come on, Amora, you need to be getting into the house anyway. And if you keep on looking at him like that, people are going to assume things."

Turning to face him and trying to hide the blush I felt creeping onto my cheeks, I chewed on the inside of my cheek, trying to calm my body down. "I don't understand, sir."

"You pups never do realize we used to be your age, feeling things that you can't comprehend; we understand these things. Being fourteen is a different age, but just worry about your studies and yourself right now, Amora. Boys are trouble, keep your firsts for your mate." Beta Adam grinned at me, giving me a wink as we walked into the packhouse. My pace had slowed as I thought about what he had said; there was no way to trick the older wolves, I realized that.

"I've never thought of boys as anything other than friends, Beta Adam." Quickening my pace to catch back up to him. Rachel was playing with his long hair as she sat there in his arms.

Beta Adam chuckled, glancing down at me and switching Rachel to the other arm, which then erupted into full-on laughter. "Amora, you don't have to pretend that he doesn't spark some attraction, because I can tell he does. The other unmated she-wolves notice him, and I know you do too."

I blushed again, but this time it seeped through, making my cheeks bright red. "I'm his friend, Beta. He is my brother's best friend, and I'm sad that he will be leaving in a few short weeks. Besides, there is no reason to become emotionally attached to someone when you each have a mate out there."

Beta Adam cocked his head to the side as I peeked up at him through my lashes. "Young lady, you are wise beyond your years, but the Goddess brings people into our lives not for shits and giggles but for reasons we do not understand. She will reveal those reasons throughout our lives, but we have to trust her."

I nodded and walked away. I didn't feel like going through the conversation that he was headed to. I would keep my firsts for my mate; this was a fact. Running up the stairs, I made my way to my bedroom to get ready. Today was Sawyer and Danika's eighteenth birthday, and curiosity was killing me.

I passed Nolen's room and peeked in—he always kept his door open unless he was sleeping. He was sitting on his bed speaking into his phone, a towel hung around his bare shoulders, and he had on grey sweatpants. The huskiness of his voice carried to my ears, and I stopped to listen.

"Mother, please don't do the party. You realize the pack won't come; I'm not Archer. Mom... Okay, fine, I will be home in a few weeks. Sawyer and Danika are turning eighteen tonight, so I'll call you afterward... Yes, mother.... I'll call you later. I love you."

I stifled a giggle, trying to sneak off before he caught me listening to his conversation.

"Are you eavesdropping?"

I stopped in my tracks and turned. Nolen stood there freshly showered in his sweatpants, his eyes roamed over my body, and at that moment, I wanted to step up to him, but instead I bit my bottom lip and smirked. "Damn, you caught me. You getting ready for the party?"

Nolen's head tilted and he cocked an eyebrow. "Yes, I wouldn't miss it for the world. Shouldn't you be getting ready?"

"Yep, on my way to my room," I answered, crossing my arms across my chest. Nolen's eyes glowed, and I realized I hadn't imagined it. They had done the same thing when he'd locked eyes with me at the challenge. "How did you do that?"

Nolen blinked and shook his head, stepping back further into his room, keeping his distance from me. "Do what?"

"You know... Never mind. I'll meet you at the party." I let it go and walked away before I said something I shouldn't, but I glanced back at him over my shoulder, his arms crossed over his muscular chest, and he gave me a wink when he caught me.

))))) ❦ (((((

Mother refused to let me wear anything but a dress. I mean, it's not like Sawyer would become Alpha tonight. So, now here I was wearing this stupid dress for his birthday party. Walking down the hall, Sawyer's door opened, and he came out with just a wifebeater and basketball shorts on. He peered down at me and then smirked. "Aw, my little sister is getting all dressed up for my birthday! One of these days, you're going to call me Alpha."

"Ha, when that day comes, hopefully I'll be mated and out of this pack." And I walked past him to the stairs. The heels killed my feet; I wasn't made for these types of shoes.

"Come on, sis, why would you want to leave the pack? You realize most mates are in the same pack. Besides, our pack is huge, and you never know if one of the warrior males will be your mate," he teased, nudging me in the arm with a grin. I ignored him, noticing Nolen in a navy-blue collared shirt and grey dress pants at the bottom of the steps. A she-wolf was rubbing up against him. My heart sank when she placed a kiss on his cheek; his hand went to the she-wolf's hand that traveled over his chest.

"Looks like someone has the green sickness." Sawyer slapped me on the back, and I glanced over at him as I tried to hold back the tears in my eyes. He wasn't mine, as much as I wanted him to be. Other she-wolves had every right to try to get his attention.

Nolen's head swung to face me; his eyes ran over the teal dress I wore, which made my heart start racing. His head cocked to the side as if he overheard my racing heart, and dismissing the she-wolf, he walked up the stairs to me. I couldn't take my eyes off him, and I thought I would faint when he gave me that gorgeous smile. He motioned over to Sawyer and held out his hand for me to take. "Ready to go? We have to be on the stage before shithead here."

Not trusting myself to speak, I nodded. I couldn't understand why I felt like this around him, but I would miss it when he left.

Taking his hand, we descended the stairs to the backyard where Sawyer and Danika would turn eighteen and shift. I sighed. I would be turning eighteen after Nolen left to go back home. Peeking up through my lashes, I tried to steal as many memories as I could before he was gone forever.

"You keep looking at me like you'll never see me again."

Removing my gaze from him, I glanced around our surroundings. I didn't want anyone to overthink our conversation. "Well, you'll be going back to your pack in a few weeks. Possibly taking over soon."

Nolen pulled me in closer to his side; there was no way he didn't feel the shiver that ran down my body as his closeness. "Yeah, I doubt I'll be taking over at all. I've told you before—my pack doesn't like me, and they will never want me to be Alpha."

We went up the stairs; I couldn't figure out why he continued to say things like this. I mean, when he came to the pack, he'd been scrawny, but it should not have been a reason he wouldn't be accepted to be Alpha. This tall, gorgeous guy beside me was everything they needed. He would lay down his life to keep his pack safe, yet the pack didn't feel the same for him. According to him.

We stopped just to the left side of my mother and father. Danika's parents stood on the other side of my parents, waiting with excited expressions on their faces. See, what was crazy was Sawyer and Danika were born minutes apart from each other. The two of them walked up the steps of the stage, and Danika went over to her parents while Sawyer stood before ours.

My father walked up to the front, and everyone in the pack became quiet; he beamed at them, all his excitement being felt within the whole pack. "Quartzite pack! Here, in just a few short minutes, these two young wolves will turn eighteen! Where they will shift for the first time and, with any luck, find their mates amongst us!"

The roar from the crowd made me smile. My pack loved one another. We all might squabble, but at the end of the day, we all made sure everyone was safe. I gazed up at the moon that slid out of the clouds. It would be a memorable night as the two wolves that were turning eighteen had been blessed with a full moon tonight.

Sawyer and Danika walked up next to my dad, and everyone became quiet when the first snap happened. Sawyer's face contorted in pain, but he made no sound. The next minute, where my brother had been standing, a massive grey and white wolf now stood. His head raised to the moon, and a long howl erupted from it.

Other howls followed him; Sawyer's cut short when his wolf's head turned suddenly to Danika. She had yet to shift, but the grey wolf never took his eyes off her. Another snap sounded, and Danika screamed before a golden-brown wolf took her place.

Its eyes went to the grey wolf's; she went up to him, rubbing her nose and head under his jaw. Sawyer's wolf started to lick Danika's face and ears. I'd had my suspicions that they were to be mates, but the mate bonds were so weird, and sometimes you couldn't predict who would be and who wouldn't be.

They finally shifted back and were handed clothes to wear. Seeing the love in their eyes made it more of my goal to have that. I mean, who wouldn't want to be loved like that? To realize no matter what, they were yours and you were theirs. I glanced back up at Nolen; this boy had turned into more of a man over the time he had been here. Making me believe things that I thought he might sense too.

My father went back up to the front, his face alight with happiness as he wrapped his arms around them both. "Meet your future Alpha and Luna! I am proud to have our Delta's daughter as my daughter-in-law! Now, let's feast!"

Everyone dispersed, and I went up to Sawyer and Danika, hugging her and then my brother. Nolen and Sawyer shared a hug, and he dipped his head to Danika. "You both look great! I'm glad that you found each other."

"Don't worry, man, here in a few short weeks, you will be eighteen, and then you will find your mate." Sawyer smiled and pretended to box with him. Nolen chuckled as he juked Sawyer's punches.

"We will see." Nolen's face held that familiar look on it when he talked about finding his mate. He really thought that he wouldn't have a chance to have a mate, to experience the love that only a mate could give you. If only I could be his, if only I could put him at ease, because deep down, I had feelings for him.

My face fell as I thought about him leaving next week, but this was not something that I needed to deal with at the moment. Plastering a smile on my face, I glanced over to Danika. "Congrats, Danika, I hope you can keep him in check. Excuse me; I'll be right back."

I left the group because I would cry over losing one of my best friends if I didn't. When I thought I had made it out of everyone's sight, I started to run up the stairs to put as much distance away from him and from the depression that began to consume me, to bring me down.

)))))🐺(((((

Nolen

I gazed at Amora as she walked away from us, and the further she went, the clicking of her heels faded away. I turned to Sawyer, and he shrugged, his arm wrapping around Danika's waist. He placed a kiss on her temple, making her giggle.

Seems Amora is upset, Nolen. Sarge was pacing in my head, making me uncomfortable as well. I wanted to follow her to find out what had bothered her.

Yeah, I saw that.

We are now the third wheel.

I turned, watching everyone at the party. Next week I would be at my pack, the wolves that I have come to call friends would be a thing of the past. I might end up seeing Sawyer and Danika, but the others I would never see again.

In a few months, everyone will know me. The wolf in my head curled up and laid down. His ears drooped. My eighteenth birthday loomed closer, and I was ready to meet Sarge, but I was unprepared for the other change. That would pull me from the people here, but it was coming, and fast.

CHAPTER NINE: RHYOLITE PACK

I told everyone goodbye other than Amora; she had not wanted to come down from her room and said she was not feeling well. Hoisting my bag over my shoulder, I gazed down the hall to where her door was closed. I sighed and walked down the stairs for the last time. This was not how I wanted to leave things with her.

The SUVs traveled down the road toward my pack; my mom and dad had sent a few warriors and Archer's third in command, Gamma Lucas, to come to pick me up. He didn't speak much to me, which was fine by me. I caught him glancing over at me a lot, but I ignored him.

He had been staring at me for the last five minutes; it seemed like he wanted to say something, since he kept starting to speak and then backtracking on it. Finally, he spit out a sentence. "So, Nolen, you've changed a lot."

I turned to him, looking at him entirely for the first time during trip. The crimson-haired young man before me was burlier than he had been when I left, but I had also gotten stronger. His light green eyes tried to hold my gaze, but I could sense Sarge pushing forward, making his inner wolf submit. "Yeah, not like I wanted to. I could have lived being in Archer's shadow."

Lucas sighed, then leaned back; he gave me a saddened glance, running his hand through his hair. "Naw, man, Archer didn't want you in his shadow. That's why he pushed you so hard. He wanted you right up there with him. This would make him proud."

I couldn't figure out what to say to that. Sitting back in my seat, I closed my eyes. Lucas had been one of the kindest members of the pack to me.

He and Archer had kept people at bay. Well, other than Axel, but that was because he was of lower rank and couldn't order Axel around.

Axel, the wolf that had tormented me behind Archer's back, now my Beta, concerned me. I understood that when I took over the reins as Alpha, he would be second in command, and all I could do was hope that he had done some growing up.

If he hasn't, we will put him in his place! Sarge snarled, his hackles raised. Shaking my head at this crazy wolf of mine, I gazed back out the window as we pulled through the gates of my pack. Lucas smiled at me and nodded to the view. "Welcome home, Nolen."

The pack had changed in the four years I had been gone. Constructions on new buildings were underway, while other finished projects stood vacant, awaiting tenants, and training pups were fighting on new training fields. The smell of sawdust and freshly cut trees was everywhere. Driving down the newly paved road, all the wolves in the center of the pack stopped to stare at the vehicles heading up to the packhouse.

We pulled up to the steps, and Lucas got out on the other side, but I couldn't bring myself to exit the SUV. Those steps had changed my life forever, where I had watched my mother hug my brother for the last time, covered in his blood as she wailed to the Goddess, who could have allowed him to live to take his rightful place as alpha.

"Come on, Nolen." Lucas stuck his head back in the SUV.

I glanced back at him, pity written all over his face. I nodded and glanced back; my father and mother stood on the steps waiting for me to join them. My father's Beta and Axel were also standing there, and I took a deep breath and opened the door.

I'm right here with you, Nolen. Sarge had his eye on Axel.

Straightening up once I dismounted the vehicle, I heard my mother squeal, and the unavoidable smile that lit up on my face encouraged her to race down the steps to me. She stopped in front of me and had to incline her head back to gaze into my face. I had missed her so much, even though we spoke on the phone often. My mother would be the only woman that would love me and be at my side. Her hands came to my cheeks, and tears built up in her eyes. "My Nolen... you have changed so much since I last saw you. You have grown so tall!"

I grinned at her and pulled her into a hug. I wanted to erase the memories that these steps held. Forget the pain, sorrow, and loss. The only way to do that was to create a new happier moment that started right here and now, with this simple hug. I held back the tears that threatened to spill from my eyes; my mother would never understand how much this meant to me.

Someone cleared their throat, pulling us from our embrace. My mother smiled at me again before grabbing my arm and walking with me up the stairs to the other males. I scanned over them, watching as their faces held various emotions. My father and the Beta's faces beamed with pride, and Axel looked like he had seen a ghost.

Father's Beta came up to me with his hand out. I grasped his firmly, shaking it. He used his other hand to clap me on the shoulder, his smile broadening. "You've filled out, little man."

I nodded with a smile, and my dad came forward, looking me over with approval. I now had a couple of inches on him. Which he thought was funny as he chuckled while he grabbed my hand. He hadn't been much of a hugger even when Archer was alive.

"What did they feed you there? You're almost as big as grandpa."

"Nothing they don't feed everyone else." I laughed while shaking his hand. My gaze went to Axel, he had become bulkier since I left, but he was six years older than me. He hadn't changed much in the four years of my training. His blond hair was short, and his green eyes stared at me, taking me in, which I assumed he was doing to see if he could still make my life miserable. When he locked eyes with me, he quickly dropped them. His face had claw marks on one side, down below his jaw. They must've been recent since they hadn't been there when I left.

Axel and Lucas hung back as we headed into the packhouse. One of the omega's had come and gotten my stuff, running it up the stairs. They had redecorated, and everything looked new. Couches and end tables sparkled under the contemporary chandelier, the walls were freshly painted, and grey curtains hung loosely on their rods.

I spotted a group of she-wolves trying to hide as they peeked around the corner in one of the halls. Giggling erupted from them when they caught me glancing their way. Ignoring them, I followed my dad to his office. All the she-wolves would hear of my arrival here in the next few hours.

My father opened the door, and we all filed in, where he went and sat behind his desk. My mother and I sat down on the love seat, and the Beta, Axel, and Lucas took the chairs. We all waited for my father to start talking. My mother kept her hand on my forearm as though she had to remind herself that I had really returned to her.

I took a deep breath before turning to my father—he, apparently, wasn't going to be the first to talk, and the atmosphere in the room was becoming suffocating. "Is there a reason you brought us to your office? You only bring people here if it's important."

"It's because it is important, Nolen. You will be turning eighteen here in the next few weeks. We are going to set up a party, and I know that you don't like parties, but this is important, you will be shifting for the first time, and I feel like we need to celebrate that." My father sat in his chair, waiting for my reply. I knew when mother called at the Quartzite pack this wouldn't have been dropped. There was no way I could think about getting out of this.

"Sweetheart, we can invite the Quartzite pack! I know you have made lots of friends over there, including Sawyer. I hear he found his mate!" My mother turned between my father and me. Her hand squeezed mine, bringing my attention fully to her, which then started me thinking. If we invited the Quartzite pack, that would mean Amora would come, right?

All I could think about was the potential of seeing her again, and if a party would bring her to me, then I would do anything to see her. Glancing over to my mother, I nodded to her in agreement. "Yeah, that's fine. What's life without a little fun?"

My father's hand cupped his chin as he thought it all over. At first, I thought he would say no. He then glanced over at me and stood from his chair, leaning on his hands. "I don't see why we couldn't invite the Quartzite pack. Go on up to your room and settle in. We will deal with everything."

I stood up, and I could tell the difference in their demeanor toward me. Nodding to my parents and then the Beta, I walked out of the room. Making my way down the hallway, I heard footsteps behind me; I knew it was Axel before turning to go up the stairs. Our eyes met as I stood on the second step, which made me tower over him even more. "Is there something you want to say to me?"

Axel shifted on his feet and ran his hand through his hair. I could see the beads of sweat on his forehead as he finally glanced up at me. "Nolen, I know I wasn't the best person to you, and I have a lot of things to make up for. I know that I'm not your first choice as your second, but I can promise that I can do this job."

I stared at him as he shifted nervously in place as I continued to make eye contact with him. Letting him and his wolf know that I wouldn't be bullied by him again.

"Yeah, you have a lot to make up for and prove for me to be able to trust you. If for any reason I doubt your ability to put this pack and me above yourself, I will replace you."

The shocked look on Axel's face turned to determination as he bowed his head to me. I nodded back and proceeded up the stairs to my room.

The weeks passed by reasonably fast. I continued my training, and our Beta learned that putting me one-on-one with others my age was not the best idea. He started pairing me up with older wolves who had experience, and their wolves. Even then, he would have to put two against me to make it fair.

The pack that once teased and bullied me now gazed at me in amazement. They all surrounded me during my sparing sessions and stared at me each time I took down more experienced wolves in the ring. But they wouldn't come near me or speak to me; each one would submit when I came near.

When I had walked through the grounds after I got back home that day, many wolves had stopped what they were doing and stared at me. I'd kept my gaze from lingering on them too long as I took in the new buildings and the ones being remodeled.

I had continued through the small town, taking in the beauty of the changing leaves. Riddled with pines and oaks, the forest kept the patrol wolves hidden as they ran through the underbrush at the boundary line. Galloping feet echoed through the trees, making my heart race with them. I couldn't wait to be able to be out there running as Sarge.

I love this place, my favorite place to clear my mind. Sarge's ears were forward, his nostrils flaring like he could smell the forest scents.

You will be running these lands soon.

My father had sent an invitation to the Quartzite pack, and they were coming tonight for my birthday tomorrow. This was the only reason I had agreed to even have a party—to have the chance to see Amora again. That was, if she decided to come, which was my prayer that she would.

I walked into Archer's old room; my parents had not touched it since he died. I liked to go there to think when I needed to step away from everything. This was my safe place, the place I could come when my mind needed to get away from everything.

The room still held a hint of his scent. Pictures of him and his friends sat on his dresser, and a picture of him and I sat in front of all the other images.

I felt like he was still with me when I stood in his room. Looking around the space, I detected that only my scent was there, along with his fading one. My footprints in the dust were littered throughout the room where I walked around, pacing, thinking about the times I had with Archer.

"Nolen, are you in here again?" I heard Archer say as he opened his door.

I sat there at his desk when he came up to me. I looked up at him with a grin. My brother had started to grow a five o'clock shadow on his jaw, and the un-mated females loved him even more for it. His blue eyes showed excitement as he gazed down at me. We could have been twins, but it was only our facial features, eyes, and hair that were the same. I had always been scrawny and seemed to have been starved all my life, even though I ate more than my brother.

"Are you going to get ready? It's about time for my eighteenth birthday party." Archer placed his hand on my shoulder and gave it a squeeze. He would shift and then find his mate tonight. He was lucky; when it became my turn, the she-wolf would reject me because I wasn't desirable.

"Yeah, just sitting here thinking." The thing with my brother was he always knew when I wasn't myself. There was no hiding anything from him, nothing. Which was probably how he'd figured out I was being bullied by the wolves my age before he had walked in on the shower scene.

"Thinking about what, Nolen?" His eyes were soft as they gazed down on me. He never judged me, but he pushed me harder than Dad did. I never understood why he was going to become alpha, and Axel, Lucas, and Daylen would help him lead the pack.

I rose from the desk and went to his window, gazing at the commotion of the decorators as they fixed up the backyard of the packhouse. All those wolves down there were excited about the party and the possibility of learning who their new Luna would be. "Am I always going to be like this? What if I never receive the respect you have?"

Archer draped his arm around me and chuckled a little as he stood there with me, staring at the busy wolves two stories below. "You will, Nolen. Because you know what they say about the runt of the litter?"

I glanced up at him and shook my head no. His eyes met mine, a grin spread over his lips, and he gave me a wink. "They always turn out to be the biggest and strongest!"

I smiled at Archer. He was six years older than me, but he and I were the best of friends. He always made sure that everyone stayed away from me, and I was grateful for that, though most of the time I stayed in my room.

He never told Mom or Dad why I looked the way I did after being attacked, but he made sure to let the wolf know that if it happened again, there would be no mercy. If Archer ever left me, I would be in big trouble.

"Come on, little bro. Go get dressed. I need you there beside me when I shift for the first time."

A soft knock pulled me back from my memory, and I turned to the door as it opened. My mother stood there at the entryway, her hand covering her mouth as her eyes shifted around the room. Since Archer passed, she had not been in this room, and I knew her seeing me in here threw her off. I went up to her and backed her away from the door, closing it behind me. "Did you need me, mother?"

She looked between me and Archer's door before her hazel eyes met mine; tears were building there before she fought them back and gave me a faint smile. Her hand came up to my cheek, caressing it. "Yes, dear, the Quartzite pack has arrived."

I nodded to her and placed my arm around her shoulders. Excitement washed over me at the thought of Amora being here. They didn't say who all was coming, but I was praying to Selene that she would show. "Then let's go welcome them."

We strolled down the hall and descended the stairs to the foyer. Laughter floated up, and that's when her scent made it to me. *She came*, and it took everything in me not to hasten my steps to stand beside her.

My mother and I turned the corner and saw Sawyer and Danika talking with my dad and his Beta. I grinned when I realized they had marked each other. He never let things stew; he took life by the ears and made it work.

Sawyer's head twisted around; his grin widened when his eyes landed on me. He unwound his hand from Danika's and strolled up to my mother and me. He held out his hand when we met up, and I grasped it tightly, pulling him into a hug, "Thanks for coming, Sawyer. At least I'm familiar with someone who will be at my first shift."

Sawyer laughed as we pulled away, glancing over me. "We are brothers now! I would never miss your first shift. Plus, I get to find out who your mate is!"

See, Nolen, you are not alone this time! Sawyer, Danika, and Amora are here to keep you from shifting alone.

I shifted my feet. That was one of the reasons I did not want to have this in front of the pack. If my mate was here in this pack, I could see the disgust in her eyes now. "Let's not get too carried away. We don't know if she is even here."

Sawyer nodded and then bent closer to my ear, "And I can't wait to meet this wolf of yours. Mine is excited as well; Torak knows we are good friends and wants to be good friends with him."

I nodded to him, trying to find Amora in the crowd without letting everyone know I was looking. When I spotted her, she was with a few of her friends, talking. A male from my pack walked over and started to speak with them. I continued to gaze around, noting the different wolves that had come from the pack I had spent four years of my life with. I couldn't help but smile; the other wolves that lived in my pack looked on at the ones from the Quartzite pack, unsure of what to make of them as they all meandered around the room.

The male who walked up to Amora was still talking with her as she conversed with her friends. I glanced over to Sawyer, and we strolled over to Danika, who was still talking with my dad and his Beta. My mother followed us, and Sawyer's and Amora's parents came over.

"Nolen, you are looking great!" Alpha Roman came up to me and clapped me on my back. I grinned at him and nodded; he had always been good to me while I was staying with his pack.

"Yeah, he has put these experienced wolves through their paces. I need to talk to Beta Adam and find out what he has been teaching him," Father's Beta spoke, glancing over at the other Alpha.

"Beta Adam would be pleased to hear from you." Alpha Roman nodded to my father's Beta.

I kept my eyes on the group Amora and her friends were in with the male from my pack. He continued to place his hands on her, and she continued to shrug the male off her. She turned on him, pushing him away from her, his face turned furious, and before I knew it, I stood in-between Amora and the male wolf. The entire room fell quiet as they watched, waiting to find out what would happen. "Is there a reason you want to keep placing your hands on someone who doesn't want to be touched?"

The wolf glanced up at me, then bowed his head. "Sorry, Nolen. It won't happen again."

Sarge kept pushing to the front while I tried to keep him at bay. The wolf in front of me whimpered and turned away to head out of the room. The wolves in the room resumed their conversations after the wolf took off. Taking a deep breath, I turned to Amora, and when my eyes locked with her amber color ones, I knew I had lost myself in them again. Amora smiled up at me and then giggled. "Well, my knight in shining armor, here to protect me again."

"I hope you are doing well. And I'm sorry about that wolf." I couldn't help but be mesmerized by her, and her scent was more potent than before I'd left to come back home.

"Yeah, I'm still the same as I was before you left. But Sawyer's been whining about you not being there when Danika isn't around him." Her beautiful orbs held mine in their depths. I could live in her eyes for the rest of my life.

"Sawyer has always been a bit of a whinner," I teased, pulling my gaze from hers to glance back at Sawyer and Danika. They were talking with my mother and father, and Sawyer had my mother in fits of laughter. There was no telling what he was saying to her.

The soft-touch of her hand on my arm brought my attention back to her. Amora smiled and then glanced back over her shoulder. She turned back to me and wrapped her arm through mine. "Come on, Nolen. I think my family wants us over there."

I let her lead me through the wolves from both packs. Every once in a while I heard soft growls around me. My eyes would cut to the she-wolf that it came from. Most dropped their gaze, but others were bold enough to flirt with me. I ignored them. When we came up to our families, I became aware that Danika's and Sawyer's eyes had frosted over, and a grin had plastered itself on his face.

My father shifted his gaze between Amora and me before they landed back on Alpha Roman. "Let's get your pack to sleeping quarters, and Nolen can take Sawyer, Danika, and Amora to their rooms."

Nodding to my dad, I motioned to Sawyer to follow me. "Follow me, guys. You all will be on the top floor with my family."

Sawyer walked beside me, and Amora dropped back to talk with Danika. Sawyer nudged me as we made our way to the staircase. I already knew what he was going to ask me because he had done so many times. "So, are you ready for tomorrow? You get to shift and find your mate."

I shook my head as we made our way up the stairs. We walked past my parents' room and the room Alpha Roman and his Luna would stay in, then passed mine and then Archer's old room. I stopped at the door after Archer's and turned to Sawyer and Danika. "You both can stay in this room."

Danika walked in, but Sawyer stayed beside me, his hand on my shoulder as he held my gaze. "Nolen, relax about tomorrow. Whoever your mate is, when she knows she's yours, she will fall at your feet."

"Is that how you got me?" Danika's voice rang out from inside the room; Sawyer grinned and went to join her, closing the door behind him.

Amora giggled beside me, bringing my attention back to her. Goddess, I missed her these past few weeks, and after today I didn't know when I would see her again. My heart constricted at the thought of this being the last time. "She has changed him a lot."

"Yeah. Having that kind of love is something to strive for." I turned from their door and led Amora to her room across the hall right next to mine. "Well, this is your room for the time being."

She opened the door and stepped in. I stared at her as she took in the light-yellow room. She walked up to the door that connected my room to this one. My heart began to race, thinking that she would try to open the door. Amora turned back to me, her hand on the knob. "Where does this go to?"

Running my hand through my hair, I glanced down at my feet, trying to figure out what to actually say to her. I didn't want to lie to her, but there was no way I could tell her that it was unlocked. "My room. It's locked on the other side, and it can be locked on this side as well."

I glanced back up to her, my heart racing since the door had not been locked in a very long time, and I hoped she did not test it. She turned to me with a smile and resumed walking around the space. The way the afternoon sun played upon her features made her skin glow. "This room is pretty. I can't wait to see your wolf, Nolen."

"Yeah, it's going to be a wild night tomorrow." I stepped further into the room, my back facing the door that connected my room to hers. Watching her wander about, I couldn't help but follow her with my eyes.

She came back up to me, her eyes holding mine captive as they always did. This girl in front of me made me feel light on my feet. The way she pulled her bottom lip between her teeth had me aching. "You might even meet your mate."

"Yeah," She stood right in front of me. I reached up to her face and tucked her hair behind her ears. Amora's lips parted, and her eyes dropped from mine to my lips. Her tongue wet her bottom lip before she pulled it in between her teeth again.

Both my hands cupped her face, and her soft hands went to my waist. I knew she wanted to save all her firsts for her mate, but her presence weakened my resolve. Amora's body pressed against mine; our breath mingled together; my lips were about to touch hers when her hands went to my chest, pushing away from me.

Dejection swept through me until I felt the presence of another person in the room. Turning, I found my mother in the doorway, her hand on her chest and a bright smile on her face, giving us a side-eye. The joy that lit up her features made me realize she had seen the whole thing. "What are you two doing in here?"

CHAPTER TEN: SARGE

AMORA

My heart was still racing after Nolen and his mother left my room. He walked out without saying anything to me. Which had me confused, and it puzzled me even more that I had not tried to stop him from kissing me. I wanted him to kiss me, and I would have let him, even though I didn't want to compare anything to my mate. If Nolen's mother had not been in the doorway, I don't know what would have happened. She'd seemed excited that she had caught us about to kiss.

I walked into the bathroom and started to take a shower. Stripping out of my clothes, I turned on the water and stepped into the warm spray. Why was I so drawn to him? I mean, I was only fifteen; there was no way to feel the mate bond right now. I washed and then stepped out of the shower, wrapping a bath sheet around my body.

Walking out of the bathroom, I noticed my bag had been carried up and was sitting by the bed. Making my way over to it, I glanced over to the door that linked my room to Nolen's. He'd said it was locked on his side. Dropping the towel, I stood naked beside the bed while I riffled through the duffle bag. I pulled out a pair of shorts and a tank top and got dressed.

I gazed back to the door, wondering if I should lock it on my side, deciding not to. I placed my bag on the ground and climbed into the bed under the quilt. Lying there looking up at the ceiling, the almost kiss still on my mind from earlier kept me from falling asleep. His phantom hands on my face sent shivers through my body. I sat up, pushed the covers off, and got up.

Creeping up to the door separating our rooms, I tried the knob, and to my surprise, it opened. *He said it was locked on his side.* My heart started beating in my chest as I opened the door. His scent overwhelmed my senses as I peeked into the room. The soft rhythmic breath sounds coming from the bed told me that he was in a deep sleep.

I decided to go back to bed, but before I turned to shut the door, my foot landed on a squeaky board. Glancing back to Nolen's bed, I thought his eyes flashed open. Closing the door back, I returned to bed.

Tomorrow was going to be exciting. I would see my friend shift to his wolf.

)))))🐺(((((

The sun shone brightly through my window, waking me from my slumber. I opened my eyes and surveyed the room, panicking a little since the dream I'd had seemed so real. Sitting up in the bed, my breathing was rapid as the adrenaline left my system. I ran my fingers through my long tresses, working out any of the knots I could before brushing it. Glancing over to the door that connected my room to Nolen's, I sighed. I hadn't locked my side of the door, why—I had no earthly idea.

Throwing the cover off me and getting up out of bed, I made my way over to the vanity and plopped down, a sigh escaping my lips. I gripped the brush and began running it through my light brown hair, tugging out the rest of the knots that my fingers had failed to find. A knock sounded on my door, bringing my attention to the opposite wall. "Come in."

The door opened, and Danika walked in. She smiled at me and came up behind me, placing her hands on my shoulders. She was already dressed in a long grey and teal dress; it had a deep plunging neckline. Danika had always been a beautiful girl, her long dark brown hair reached her waist, and her chocolate eyes drew you into them. I wanted to be just like her, a wonderful person and a loving mate. "Your mother told me to come in to make sure you were up. But since you are, I figure I can help get you ready."

Glancing at Danika through the mirror, I nodded to her. She smiled at me and started to work on my hair. My mind wandered over everything. The feelings I felt toward Nolen, the way he acted around me, and the dream. "Danika, did you feel different with Sawyer before your eighteenth birthday?"

"No, not really. I mean, who wouldn't be attracted to your brother? Why do you ask?" I shook my head with a frown as she continued to shape my hair into something beautiful. What could this be? This pull to him, and my Goddess—that dream! Glancing back up at Danika, I stared at her expressions as she tucked strands of hair into the updo that she'd constructed. "I had a weird dream last night."

"Oh really? What was it about?" Her gaze never moved from my hair.

"Well, it started out I was running in the woods. Like I was searching for something. As I continued to search, I saw a figure, and something told me that I needed to go to that person. I was almost there when the figure turned around; its eyes glowed. You know, like when your wolf is at the surface? Before it turned, shifted, and ran away. I tried to follow, but the wolf was too fast, and when I reached the point where it had been, I felt like I had lost part of myself. I then saw another figure, and it seemed to be laughing. Making my skin crawl. Is that not weird?"

Danika was silent as she surveyed her work on my hair. She then nodded and regarded me through the mirror. "It is a little, but do you think it may be your mate who's the figure you're chasing after? I don't know about the other one, though. Anyway, your hair is done. What are you going to wear tonight?"

I shrugged my shoulders as I gazed at myself in the mirror. She'd done a fantastic job on my hair, which made me wish that I had an older sister. But I guess, since she was mated to my brother, she was now more my sister than ever before. She grinned at me before she went to my bag, digging through the items of clothing that I'd brought with me. "I don't think I brought anything too fancy since I won't be on the stage this time."

"But you will be with us in the box. I'll be right back. I think I have something you can wear." Danika walked out the door, leaving it open.

I glimpsed someone walking past the opening. Slowly making my way across the room, I peeked out, glancing each way down the hall before I saw Nolen coming out of his room. He looked over at me and grinned, I waved at him, and he made his way to me. My mind was racing as I stared at this gorgeous wolf coming toward me.

He stopped before me, and his eyes took in the outfit that I had slept in the night before. Luckily Danika had fixed my hair; otherwise, he would have seen my bedhead. "Happy Birthday, Nolen."

"Thanks. I'm happy you came to my party. I mean you and your family." Nolen kicked his feet as he ran his hand through his styled hair, messing it up. He was wearing regular clothes at the moment. A cotton shirt and a pair of Eddie Bauer shorts. He had freshly showered, and the scent of his shampoo attacked my sinuses as he continued to run his hand through his hair. "I wouldn't miss it. I'm sorry I didn't tell you goodbye the day you left."

Nolen nodded before he let his gaze roam my form again, taking in my sleepwear. I was glad I'd showered last night. "It's okay. I didn't want to say goodbye to anyone. It was hard enough to say bye to your brother. Um... Your hair is nice."

I hadn't thought I could keep my composure if I had tried to send him off back to his pack. I had contemplated on not coming today. But I had to see him again; something inside of me had urged me to go. "Thank you. I'm not ready yet; Danika should be back any moment. She said she had something for me to wear."

I tried to turn when his hand clutched mine, bringing my attention back to him. His expression was pained as he held onto my hand. "Amora... I'm sorry about last night. I don't know what was going through my mind."

"What do you mean? Nothing truly happened," I told him, searching his eyes with mine. I felt my heart break a little with his apology, because it meant he hadn't wanted to kiss me, right?

"The kiss? Or, actually, the almost kiss. I know you've told people you are waiting. So, I'm sorry." Nolen fidgeted as he ran his hand through his hair again, making it appear as if he had just woken up.

"Oh! It's okay, Nolen. I do want to wait. But I don't think I would have regretted it though." Peeking up at him through my lashes, I didn't know why I told him the last bit; it's not like he wanted me or anything. His eyes flashed the color I had seen at the sparring match, before he tilted his head to the right.

I glanced over, and Danika was stopped in the middle of the hall watching our encounter, a slight smile on her face making me blush. Glancing back up to Nolen, his eyes were back to their normal blue that pulled me in. "I'll let you get ready. See you in the backyard later. Thanks again for coming; it means a lot."

Nolen winked at me and then strolled back down the hall, passing Danika with a nod in her direction. Danika came up to me, her smile broad. She turned me around into the room and steered me toward the bathroom, a lavender piece of cloth draped over her arm. "I think you have a crush!"

"No, I don't. He's one of my friends." Glancing over at her from the corner of my eye, I watched as she laughed at me. Did I really have a crush on him? Had I let myself fall for someone who wasn't my mate?

"Okay, keep telling yourself that." She continued to guide me to the restroom as I reached for a pair of panties on the bed. Oh shit! Had Nolen seen my underwear on the bed? "Here, go in there and try this on. I'm sure it will fit you."

Nodding, I took the garment she handed me and entered the bathroom. Turning to the mirror, I gazed at myself in the tank top and shorts. Goddess, why did you let me stand there in this in front of him? I must have looked goofy as hell. Placing the outfit Danika gave me on the counter, I dropped the shorts and replaced them with the black lace underwear I had brought into the small, tiled room. I tugged off the tank top, my breasts freed from the cloth that bound them.

I grabbed the outfit, stepped into it, pulled it up, and slipped my arm in the single strap. Smoothing the wrinkles out, I then looked up. The Fuchsia jumper fit me perfectly; the pants clung to my butt and thighs but widened after the knee. Its top had a single sleeve that opened in the middle before a sash tied around my waist, completing the look.

The color complimented my skin tone, and I fell in love with it as soon as my eyes landed on it. I turned and stepped out of the bathroom; Danika gave me a whistle as she fixed her hair and makeup at the dressing table in my room. I blushed and sat down on the bed as I dug through my bag to find my black stilettos. Seeing them, I slipped them on and stood up.

"So, what all is planned for today?" I turned in my heels to the vanity mirror and glanced at Danika as she finished up. Would Nolan notice me? I was still modest in all respects of the word. Nothing like what I'd seen some of the other She-wolves wear to a shift.

"I'm pretty sure the males are doing some guy things that they think are cool until the actual party. But the females are all still getting ready." Danika lifted her gaze to me in the mirror, a smile playing on her lips.

I glanced around the room and spotted a clock. It was only noon, so I still had hours before Nolen shifted. What would I do until then? My stomach growled at that exact moment, rumbling at me. "So, what are we going to do?"

"I figure we could watch the guys before the festivities. Sawyer has been asking me when I will be done getting ready for hours now." She laughed as she placed the last bobby pin in her hair. Danika smiled at me through the mirror, turning her head from side to side. "Come on. First, we need to find something to eat. I'm starving."

I nodded and waited for her to stand up from the vanity. We left my room, making our way to the dining room. The floor we were on was decorated as well; music could be heard throughout the house. The aroma of different types of food floated up to me, and my stomach rumbled louder, making Danika laugh at me.

Wolves were still busy placing decorations everywhere in the packhouse. I was excited that Nolen would finally have a party fit for an alpha at his pack. He truly deserved it, with as much stuff as he had gone through before coming to my pack. We reached the end of the steps and started down the first-floor hallway to the dining room.

Some doors on the first floor were open, revealing the she-wolves in them getting ready. Each one wore a dress that barely covered anything on their body. I guess they were hoping to be Nolen's mate and Luna. None of them deserved him. He was too good for them and their backstabbing ways. They only wanted him because he was now in line for the title and was no longer the scrawny little boy they'd bullied. I felt Danika's hand on my shoulder, bringing my attention to her. "Amora, are you okay? You look a little pissed."

Shaking my head to her question, I continued to the dining room. I had no grounds to be upset with these females who wanted to hope that they were Nolen's mate. I mean, if I were of age, I'd hope too! But I wasn't; being three years younger kept me from finding my mate, and Nolen would find his mate tonight. I had contemplated asking him to choose me, and I don't know why. Probably because I had fallen for him when I shouldn't have. Nolen needed to have his fated mate to be able to grow stronger, to be able to be stronger, and he would not get that with a chosen mate.

Danika and I walked into the dining room, and I spotted Sawyer and Nolen talking to his parents. They were both in Ts and shorts; Nolen's muscles rippled with each movement. The dining room had been set up with streamers and balloons. A long table sat upfront with Nolen's and my parents sitting there, with Nolen and Sawyer standing in front of them. We sat down on my parents' other side, and I glanced over at Nolen. He was staring at me, his eyes roaming over me. As he noticed my outfit, heat rushed through my body, and Nolen gulped when our eyes connected. I grinned at him, and he smiled back. His stare gave me confidence that he liked what he saw, making my body heat up more and my nipples to get hard. Damn it, I didn't have a bra on.

A few omegas brought us some food, and we both thanked them. I began to eat, when Sawyer and Nolen turned and left the dining room. Watching them walk out of sight, I brought my gaze back to my plate, silently wishing he would have stayed and had lunch with me.

I had not seen Nolen since the dining room. But it was now time to start his party, Danika and I made our way to our box. Sawyer and my parents would be on stage with Nolen and his parents. I was excited but also frightened since I would be losing him forever once he locked eyes with his mate. I would be a thing of the past.

Beta Adam joined us in the box, and I glanced nervously around the crowd. Surprisingly enough, females from his pack were among the ones dressed up. She-wolves were adorned with all kinds of jewelry and make-up, trying to impress Nolen. Some gave each other dirty looks while others celebrated with their friends. It was getting closer to when Nolen would turn eighteen, and I knew he would be nervous coming out in front of the pack. He had told me countless times when we were alone.

As both my parents and Nolen's walked through the crowd, everyone became quiet. The four of them were dressed in nice business casual wear. Sawyer walked out with Nolen, who had changed since I saw him at lunch, and I could tell he was nervous as his eyes scanned the crowd. They both walked up on stage, and Alpha Nero came forward, smiling at everyone. Nolen stood tall next to my brother, and I couldn't have been more proud of him at that moment.

"Rhyolite pack, it's almost time to celebrate Nolen's eighteenth birthday! And we may even find out who will be our next Luna!"

A few of the un-mated she-wolves squealed while others stood there glancing at each other. Nolen's father turned to him, motioning him forward. Nolen moved to his side. He wore a pair of gym shorts and a tank top; his tattoo peeked out of the shirt.

He glanced up at me and seemed to relax a little bit. That's when a loud snap resounded through the air. Nolen's face contorted in pain, but he didn't make a sound. His eyes changed to a deep golden color as fur sprouted from his body and more snaps sounded out. My breath hitched with each snap of bone as Nolen transformed into his wolf.

The wolf that had taken Nolen's place was massive; it was black with a grey underbelly. Gasps came from the crowd, and when his head turned in my direction, I felt my heartbeat rapidly in my chest. Those eyes made me weak, and I couldn't tear mine away from them. If this was happening before my eighteenth birthday, I could only imagine what a real bond would feel like.

Nolen

After I shifted, her scent became unbearable to not glance at her. Oh! And when I did, I got lost in her eyes! She was the one, my mate! But because she was not of age, I would not be able to claim her. I could handle that, because when she turned eighteen, I knew she would accept me.

I turned Sarge's massive head from her and glanced at my mother and father, tilting my head. It took everything in me to keep from running to her, gathering her up in my arms, and taking us away from this crowd. I had to make it seem that my mate was not here for the time being, and then after the party, I would tell my mother and father.

My mother was crying, and I quickly shifted back as Sawyer brought me another pair of shorts. Pulling them on, I went to my mother and hugged her. "Mother, what's wrong? Everything is going to be okay."

Sobbing into my chest, she looked up at me, "Your brother didn't find his mate when he shifted. Your wolf and his look exactly the same! If this is an omen, I can't take it!"

I looked up from her to my father, his face had fallen, and I shifted my gaze to Sawyer's parents; their solemn faces did not help. Turning to Amora, her face brightened from the frown she had moments ago when I'd pulled my eyes from hers. I grinned at her and then shifted my gaze to Beta Adam. He stood there, his arms crossed over his chest, and gave me a curt nod with a hint of a grin. I nodded back to him, bringing my attention back to my mother.

Taking her face in my hands, I made her look at me. I stared into her hazel eyes for a few seconds to make sure she was paying attention to me. "Mother, I swear to you that I will not leave you. You will not have to live this life without me."

She nodded, and I brought her back into the hug. My father stepped forward, placing his hand on my shoulder as he turned to the pack. "Rhyolite pack! I give you your future, Alpha!"

The pack cheered at the announcement of my future role.

After my shift, the real party started. I tried to stay as far away from Amora as possible, but her scent kept stalking me. Every unmated male in my pack made a move on her, which made me fight to keep Sarge from making me shift and tearing them apart. I couldn't really blame them. I mean, come on, the outfit she had on hugged her curves, and the color looked amazing on her.

I don't understand why you don't go and tell them to keep away from what is ours! Sarge growled at me, his ears back against his head.

We have been over this. She is still too young to know, and I don't want to sway her, I calmed him, looking back at Amora and the male beside her. He was one of the warrior wolves, and he was fearless for going up to the daughter of an alpha. Tonight would be tough to get through. She was beautiful; there was no denying that, and she was mine. Well, in three years, that is.

"Nolen! Are you okay? You have been staring over there at my sister and her friends for a long time." I glanced back over to Sawyer and Danika. They both shared a glance before returning their eyes to me. Damn, people were starting to notice. This was not good.

"Yeah, I'm not too sure about that wolf next to them," I told them, turning my gaze back to Amora and the male wolf. Trying to make it seem I was trying to protect all the females in that group and not just a particular one

"Nolen, do you think that we can talk with you?" My gaze landed on Axel, Lucas, and Daylen. I was still unsure how Axel would be once I was in the Alpha position. He was standing in front of Lucas and Daylen as they flanked him. Which was naturally what they all would do when I stepped into my role.

I turned to them, Sawyer at my flank; he still had doubts about Axel, after what I'd told him he had done when I was younger. "What is it?"

Axel bowed his head to Sawyer and Danika and then to me. Lucas and Daylen kept their eyes lowered from my gaze. "I just wanted to let you know that we will do anything to keep you safe. I will personally not make the same mistake twice."

I stood there, watching him; Axel kept his eyes lowered and his head bowed. Sighing, I ran my hand through my hair. One of these days, I would have to learn to trust him, and to do that, I would have to start at some point. "Axel, raise your head. We will be running this pack together once I take over. And as long as you keep the promise you just made, we will run it in harmony."

Axel brought his gaze up to meet mine and nodded, determination painted across his face, along with some sadness. "My last breath will be to protect you and this pack. And the Luna when she is found."

CHAPTER ELEVEN: VISITS

My wolf training started the following morning. I woke up early because I hadn't gotten much sleep that night. It was a mistake putting Amora in the bedroom next to mine, but how could I have known she was to be my mate? Not like I would change it if there was a way. Call me a glutton for punishment, I guess.

Sarge sighed in my head; his golden eyes now glowed in my mind. I finished getting ready and trying not to open the door that connected our rooms. Amora would still be asleep, and if I walked in there, she would think I was a creep.

You can never tell... she may welcome you, Sarge said to me while he lay down inside my head.

You are one bad wolf. You realize she is underage. And the pack laws say you can't claim someone underage.

Whining, Sarge sunk lower down in my mind, his ears droopy. *I know. But maybe she feels something. I know you felt the connection that night. She felt something when we changed.*

I had sensed the connection, but I didn't know if it was my side of the mate bond or hers and mine connecting. Her heart rate had increased when our eyes met, but other than that, she'd done nothing else to show me her side had connected to mine. So now I had to wait for her eighteenth birthday so she would realize I was hers.

On my way out of my room, her bed moved, making me stop and listen closer. She moved again, and I couldn't help but walk to the door. I tried the knob, thinking she would have locked it on her side, but it was unlocked. My heart started to beat faster as I softly opened the door. Maybe she did feel the connection?

Her scent took over my senses, and I felt Sarge come to the front of my mind. I glanced over to her, sleeping soundly on the bed, but she murmured in her sleep. Against my better judgment, I stepped further into the room, toward her lying on the bed.

Kneeling down, I laid my head on the edge of the bed beside her. I realized I was being a creep, but I couldn't help it. I needed to be as close as I could to her before she left. My eyes swept over her passive face as she lay there. Her soft breath lulled me to sleep. I would make sure no one came in this room to clean; I would need her scent until I could have her fully.

"Nolen?"

My head shot up when I noticed her eyes on me as she lay there. She didn't seem surprised or creeped out that I had my head on her bed. "Sorry, I'll leave."

I decided to stand, my hand on her bed to help push myself up, making the bed dip under my weight, when she reached out, grasping hold of my arm. Her hand touched my bare skin and I had to stifle a moan from the way the sparks from her bare skin stroked mine. Her amber eyes seemed to beg me to stay, but I knew I would tell her everything if I did. "I need to go train. Just wanted to say goodbye since I figure you'll be gone before I return."

Standing over her, she kept the quilt up to her collar bone. The spaghetti straps of her shirt showed, her eyes pleading with mine. I couldn't figure out what she was begging me for. "You'll be at my shift, right?"

I peered back into her eyes and gave her a wink. Nothing could keep me from that day. "Of course. I'd have to be dead to miss it!"

Amora smiled back at me, and then a frown crossed her beautiful features. "Nolen, I'm sorry you didn't find your mate. She must be in a different pack."

"It will be okay. I told you, the Goddess probably didn't make me one. So, I don't think that I will go to the other packs." I couldn't believe I was lying to her, but I had to because of the law. What a stupid law. "Well, I have to go. My father will be waiting for me."

How about we just skip training today and spend it with Amora? It is only the first day. What's one day, right? Sarge commented, waging his long bushy tail. This wolf would be the death of me; she would always get her way with him.

We can't, and you understand that. You are getting to be bad.

Not like you don't want to stay with her, he quipped back at me. Sarge was right. I would have loved to stay with her until she left. But I needed to tell my mother and father about her so that they didn't start planning on taking me to the other packs to find my "mate."

I left her room and made my way down to the dining room. I felt lighter than I had ever had in my life. Her scent lingered on my clothes, making me feel good, until I ran into Axel. He glanced over at me; his eyebrows raised as his gaze took in my appearance. His nostrils flared, picking up Amora's scent from my clothes. "What?"

Axel shrugged his shoulders as he continued walking beside me. He hung back a little at my left side, protecting my flank. "Nothing. You ready for training your wolf?"

"Yeah, I'm ready to stretch out and find out what he can do." This was my dream come true, to be able to feel the strength that Sarge possessed. To run free through the forest on four paws.

"Well, if he is anything like your brother's wolf, it's going to take a few older wolves to train with him." Sarge wagged his tail excitedly at Axel's comment. I shook my head as we both entered the dining room. It was empty save for a few other older wolves and my father. I sat down beside him, and an omega brought me a plate of food. I thanked her, and she blushed. These females were going to be the death of me. Shaking my head, I dug into the pile of food while surveying the room. My dad and his Beta talked beside me about going to the other packs to find out if my mate lived among them.

I would have to tell them today about Amora. Otherwise, they would have me running around to all the packs. I didn't want to have those poor un-mated females hoping they would be my mate. "Father, do you think I could talk with you and mother after training? It's about last night."

Turning to me, my father glanced over with a smile. He had never smiled as much around me before, and I tried not to let it get to me. "Of course, Nolen."

Nodding, I finished my food and stood up, walking away from the table. I went through the dining room doors and out of the packhouse. The wind blew past, bringing Amora's scent to me, and I glanced up to her at her balcony doors. Her eyes locked with mine. Every bit of me wanted to climb the side of the packhouse, take her in my arms, and tell her everything. Stupid law, I didn't understand why I couldn't just tell her. I didn't have to mate her or mark her till her eighteenth. Why couldn't she just know?

Are you sure you don't want to stay the morning with her? Sarge was lying down in my head, sweeping his tail from side to side.

You can tell I do! But if we are going to protect her when we can claim her, we need to be strong. You are not looking at the bigger picture here. Sighing, I glanced up again, her silhouette still there.

Then let's show her how strong we already are!

Smiling, I shook my head but let him take over. We sprinted the rest of the way off the landing and jumped, where we shifted in mid-air and landed at the bottom of the stairs on four paws—the shredded clothes falling like confetti around us. Sarge gazed back at her balcony, and she was there, leaning over the railing in her tank top and shorts. Her face was plastered with concern until she found us. Axel stood at the top of the stairs, shaking his head with a grin.

Sarge lifted his head to the moon that was still present in the sky and howled before taking off into the woods for the morning run. Other howls sounded around us. This was precisely how I imagined it would be when I ran with Sarge. He stretched out close to the ground, his big paws pounding the earth as he raced through the woods.

Wolves tried to keep up with him as he ran full speed. I sensed the excitement through our bond as we left the other wolves in the dust. We came around the bend, slowing just a little as another wolf came up beside us and nipped our flanks. Sarge turned on the grey and white wolf, pinning him to the ground until we realized this wolf could only be Sawyer.

Shifting back to my human form, the grey wolf did as well. "Damn! Sarge doesn't take any crap. Torak and I weren't expecting that!"

Chuckling, I took in my surroundings. I was sure there were other wolves in the area. Yet, I still wasn't too sure about standing here naked as a jaybird. Yes, I was self-conscious. "Yeah, well, if you would have let us know it was you, we wouldn't have attacked you."

Sawyer laughed, slapping his knee with his hand; he looked back up to me, still smiling. "Nolen, that's the whole point. You both were so in sync that you didn't even realize I was coming. That can be bad and good. You have to be careful out there, bud."

"I understand, but Sarge has been waiting to go run for years." Glancing around the woods, I tried to ensure that no other wolf was around us. But I couldn't find a scent or sight of anything.

"So, you want to race back and see who is faster?" Sawyer nudged me with a grin. I turned my attention to him and nodded. We both shifted and took off, running back to the packhouse.

Training only kept my mind off Amora while I was engaged with it. If I was studying or doing anything else, my mind drifted off to her. What was she doing? Did she miss me as much as I missed her? That would be a no because she didn't even realize I was her mate. Yet. It had been a month since my birthday, and I had told my parents Amora was my fated mate.

My mother had shouted with joy, knowing I would not be alone in running the pack one day. My father and his beta had let me drink with them. Telling me the stories of how they'd found their mates. I asked them to keep it quiet since she was still too young to feel the mate bond. Sarge whined in my head, and I swore he was a pup when it came to her.

After that month, I couldn't stand the whining anymore. So, I decided to go see her on one of my off days. I shifted, and we ran all the way to the Quartzite pack. Making it to the border I snuck in. Keeping aware of my surroundings, I made my way through the grounds. That's when I inhaled her scent. I turned to my left, and other scents mingled with hers as I made my way to her.

I couldn't believe my luck making it this far without being found by the patrols. Coming to the tree line, I spotted her sitting beside the lake her friends were swimming in. Sitting down at the edge, I gazed at her. She wore a blue bikini that covered the essentials, but damn, did it show off her curves. The sun-bronzed her skin, making it glow. Something glittered near her navel; she must have gotten it pierced. The anxiety from not seeing her in a month disappeared, my tail wagging in the dirt.

See, this does us good. We should come more often. Sarge told me as we stared at her through his eyes.

If we come too often, people are going to start to notice.

Sarge snorted, causing a few of the she-wolves to turn in our direction, Amora being one of them. She started to stand up, and that is when I knew we had to get out of there. Taking over because I knew Sarge would have just sat there, I turned us around and fled. Running back to my pack, wondering when I would see her again.

)))))❂(((((

Amora

I thought I heard something in the woods. Getting up, I crept to the tree line. I must have been imagining the aroma. Ever since I left after Nolen's birthday, I had this nagging feeling I was leaving something behind. I checked my bag multiple times and even ensured I had my phone. When I got to the tree line, his scent floated to me in the wind; I swear my mind was playing tricks on me.

Laughing to myself, I recalled when he'd jumped off the stairs outside of the packhouse and shifted in midair. I thought he was going to face plant on the concrete below, but when I got to the railing, his massive wolf stood there as the clothing rained down upon him. He had to be a show-off, and when he'd howled, I had felt it in my bones. Nolen had taken off as his beta shifted and ran after him; Sawyer even went after them. Boys always have to show off in front of a girl.

Turning back to my friends, I realized they were starting to play around in the water. Sighing, I went back to my spot and sat down. My gaze kept returning to the tree line; something inside of me wanted to follow his scent. Thinking this would have been easier away from him was only a lie. He stayed with me wherever I went.

My mother had started my Luna training two days after returning to the packhouse. I mean, it wasn't that hard, but it was a little redundant. It also cut into my training to fight, which upset me more because it made me have to work harder to catch back up the following day. If I was mated to an alpha, I hoped I would be in on the exciting stuff.

I hated not sitting in on the meetings that Sawyer got to, but luckily I still got to train with the other wolves, which was a nice break away from my mother, since she had Danika to teach as well. I couldn't be one of those Lunas like my mother who wanted nothing to do with war talk.

So now here I was, imaging Nolen's scent was near me. I couldn't take it anymore, and I got up, grabbing my bag and towel. "Hey, Sarah, I'm gonna head back to the packhouse, Okay?"

Sarah waved to me, showing me she heard me, and I left. I couldn't stay there and smell that scent. It was overwhelming and made me sort of sad. I had gotten used to his scent and often would sneak into the bedroom that he'd stayed in to help me calm down.

"Hey, Amora!"

Turning, I saw Sam, one of the pack warriors that had been tailing me ever since Nolen turned eighteen. I sighed and quickened my pace to try to keep away from him. He would always stop me and try to persuade me to go out with him.

I had tried to tell my dad, but he had more important things to deal with. I had almost made it to the steps of the packhouse when he caught up with me. "Hey! Did you not hear me?"

I turned around to face him and glared at him. "Yes, I did, but I do not want to speak with you at this time, Sam. I don't want to go on a date with you, nor do I want to spend time with you. So please leave me alone."

"Are you still stuck on Nolen? He isn't even part of our pack, and when he shifted, he didn't claim you or anyone as his mate. You know the rumors going around, and if they're true, it means his bloodline will die out." His eyes held contempt for me, and I didn't care at the moment.

"Yeah, well, I don't care! Leave me alone." Turning, I stomped off up the stairs to the packhouse doors. I passed my brother, who stood staring at Sam at the front doors as I refused to talk to him. When I made it into the house, Sawyer hadn't followed me, but at this point, I had no care in the world. Making my way to my bedroom, I slowed as I went by Nolen's old room. His scent was slowly being replaced by the omegas that cleaned the packhouse, which was expected since I had no reason to keep them out of the room.

I finally made it to my room when Sawyer got to the top of the stairs. The way he was staring at me told me it would be in my best interest not to go into my room. He crossed his arms over his chest and stood a little taller. Rolling my eyes, I copied him. "What, Sawyer?"

"When were you going to tell me about him not leaving you alone after you told him to?" Sawyer scowled at me, and it made me furious that he thought I couldn't take care of my own problems. I mean, damn, I wasn't a little pup anymore; I was one of the fiercest she-wolves in training right now.

"Because you have more important things to deal with than your sister and her problems."

"That's what an Alpha does is keeps order in the pack. If Nolen were here, you would have told him." He sighed and dropped his façade as he closed the gap between us.

Glancing up at my brother, I searched his face to try to find the answers to the questions I didn't want to ask. "Why are people even spreading those rumors? I mean, just because he didn't find his mate that night doesn't mean he won't ever find her. Right?"

Sawyer glanced away and back up the hallway before turning back to me, a solemn expression on his face. His hand ran through his hair as he stared at me. He always did this when he was uncomfortable and it sort of scared me.

"There is a prophecy," he said.

CHAPTER TWELVE: THREATS

I continued to make my weekly visits to see Amora. It started out monthly, but it tore me apart to stay away from her. During the times I visited her monthly, my training would suffer.

So there I was again at the tree line, watching her like a lovesick pup in my wolf form. Today, Amora had the radio on playing some rock music while she and her friends danced around on the patio in the back. I should have told Sawyer and his father that the patrols were not doing their jobs very well since I had been sneaking onto the territory for the past few months.

However, I didn't because they would realize I had been here to see Amora or someone on the pack lands without following the proper protocol.

As I sat there, the wind shifted, sending my scent to the group of girls. Being werewolves, even without our wolf form, we can still pick up on familiar scents. Amora's head jerked to the tree line as she searched with her eyes to define who lurked there. Her reaction made my heart jump into my throat; I hoped it meant that she missed me as much as I missed her.

Crouching in the lilies, I stayed still as her eyes searched for my scent. Eventually, she gave up and returned to the activity she and her friends were now playing. I remained low in the flowers while I surveyed her.

A twig snapped behind me, causing me to twist around, facing Torak. I took off toward our secret meadow, leading him through the underbrush until I got to the clearing. Turning, I confronted him as he came through the tree line.

He shifted, and I followed suit. "Hey, man, why didn't you tell me you were coming over. We could have talked in the packhouse."

I fidgeted in place as I sat down on one of the boulders in the meadow. The chill from the rock froze the skin that made contact with it. Sawyer tilted his head and then joined me on the other boulder. Glancing back up at him, I saw the worry in his eyes. "Can I tell you something without you killing me?"

"Of course!"

I ran my hand through my hair as I glanced away from him. This was hard; every time I told him something I had been keeping a secret from him. Which made me feel like an awful friend. "Well, I found my mate the night I shifted."

Sawyer jumped up from his seat, slapping me on the shoulder. Excitement ran across his face, which lifted my mood a bit, but when I told him who, he would probably tear me apart. "Who! And why the fuck did you not tell me?"

My gaze shifted to worry as I gazed upon my friend, knowing once I told him he would be pissed. For a moment, I thought of telling him some random name, but he was my brother from another mother, and when she turned eighteen, he would figure it out. "Your sister, Amora."

I scanned his face as it went from excitement to confusion. "What do you mean? My sister? She's not old enough to be mated. How can you be mated to her?"

"This is the reason I didn't want to tell you, and the reason I'm here. I have been coming for months, gazing at her and breathing in her scent. I can't think without coming to see her," I told him as I ran my hand through my hair. He was angry, but I couldn't deny that to him. I mean, she was his baby sister, and even though she could very well take care of herself, she didn't have to because of us.

Sawyer stepped in front of me and held his jaw as he thought. I sat there waiting for the onslaught of fury from my friend, but it didn't come. "Nolen, how do you know? Do you feel the connection?"

I nodded my head and stood up, turning my back to my friend as he paced. "I don't think she can sense it. I asked my parents about younger mates, and they told me I shouldn't sense anything until my mate was of age. But I feel the pull; hell, I felt the pull since I came here. I thought it was a brotherly thing. You know?"

He was quiet for a long time until I turned back to him. He was still staring at me like I had two heads. "So, you're mated to my sister, and she doesn't recognize it because she's not eighteen yet. Why didn't you tell her? Hell, why didn't you tell me?"

"What I don't understand is that my parents say that I shouldn't be able to sense anything, but there are pack laws that say you can't tell the younger mate. The reason I didn't tell you was I thought you might be mad at me and rip me apart."

Sawyer strolled over to me and placed his hands on my shoulders. "Nolen, what in your fucking mind told you I would be mad at you? I mean, now we will be more than best friends but real brothers! I would much rather she be mated to you than these horndog males in my pack."

Grinning at him, I knew he meant that. He'd treated me like I was part of the pack as soon as I had stepped foot on his land with my parents. Sawyer's words put me at ease, knowing that he would accept our bond. "Besides, now I don't have to worry that her mate is any other wolf around here. I'm not too sure about them or an alpha that would abuse her. You understand what I mean."

"Yeah. I'm sure the rumors will die once she can sense the bond as well."

"You've heard them as well, huh?"

"Yeah. They think my family is part of this prophecy. Just because Archer didn't find his mate and everyone thinks I don't have a mate," I told him as I walked back over to the boulder I had been sitting on.

"Don't worry about it, Nolen. Once she turns eighteen, everyone will realize you aren't. Anyway, you need to be getting back to your pack, and I'm sure your father and mother will be looking for you." Sawyer chuckled, before a howl sounded throughout the territory. Another followed, bringing Sawyer's attention to them; the pitch of them didn't seem urgent, letting me believe that it was an all-clear.

"I'll leave and let you get back to your pack. Be sure to keep an eye on Amora for me?"

"Of course, man! That's a given."

I nodded and then shifted into Sarge. We watched Sawyer as he shifted and took off away from me, and then I sprinted back to my territory.

You do realize prophecies sometimes have some truth to them?

I realize that, Sarge. But why would it apply to us when we have a mate and we cannot tell her because she's not of age?

Sarge became quiet on the run back, and just as when we'd entered the Quartzite pack, we exited it without any patrols bothering us. I was sure that Sawyer would tell them to let me be from now on anytime I decided to come to see Amora.

I raced through the woods until I came to the clearing for training. Pups stood facing each other, practicing when I stepped out of the tree line. They all stopped to stare at Sarge's massive form; some even kneeled where they stood. The confidence coming from Sarge was impressive as he held his head up high. I laughed at him as he pranced around. The sound of vehicles on the dirt road leading up to the packhouse worried me. I hadn't been told we were expecting guests. Sarge took off back through the woods to the rear of the packhouse.

We made it there before the SUVs, and shifting quickly I ran up to my room and put on some clothes. I made my way back down the stairs as my mother and father opened the front door. Walking out behind them, I noticed that the wolves that exited the vehicles were from the Dolostone pack. The pack that my father, Axel, and my brother had gone to before he died.

"I'm right here with you." I turned and saw Axel to the left and Lucas and Daylen to my right. I stood a little taller as my father went up to the Alpha from their pack. He looked over to me, his face stoic, but his eyes flickered between his and his wolf's.

"Alpha Wade, what do we owe the pleasure of this visit?"

Alpha Wade walked up to my father, grabbing his outstretched hand in the process. "I've come to talk more about the land disputes."

"It's taken you long enough to think about it." My father escorted him past us, and he kept his eyes on me as he followed my father. The coldness in his eyes urged me to keep him in sight at all times while he was here. I never looked away from his stare as he and my father went into the packhouse.

Axel stirred beside me, and I turned to him. He never took his gaze from the older alpha. "I don't trust him. It's not a coincidence that when we left his territory, we were attacked by wolves a few miles from home. I'd keep your eye on him."

"You think they are the ones who sent the wolves? Wouldn't you recognize if they had been Dolostone wolves?" I questioned him as we made our way inside behind my mother. Axel kept pace with me now as we marched inside.

"Not if he had rogues working for them. I'm not going to let him get his hands on you. You need to be kept an eye on, and you don't need to be running off." Axel walked close to me as the rest of the Dolostone pack came into the packhouse behind us. "I watch you leave every week. I don't know where, but I know you leave the territory."

Turning on him, I glared at him. Sarge's will pushed further to the surface. "If I remember correctly, Axel, I'm the alpha, and you will not be giving me orders. If I want to leave the territory, I will."

Axel lowered his gaze from mine; a whimper crossed his lips as he bared his neck to me. "I understand, Nolen. But I will not let you die on me, I made my promise to keep you alive, and that is what I'll do."

I growled before turning my back on Axel and following my father and the older alpha to his office. I may not be the reigning Alpha yet, but I would not be told what I could and could not do by Axel.

I reached my father's door and walked in without knocking. Yeah, it was a power move on my part, but I knew my dad wouldn't have minded. Both Alpha's glanced up at me, and my father motioned me forward to his desk. Alpha Wade continued to stare at me from the corner of his eye as he and my father talked about the land separating his territory from ours. I sat in one of the chairs in his office, listening to them.

It didn't seem that they were getting anywhere with the land disputes. I didn't perceive this ending tonight, and definitely not soon. A knock came upon the door, and whoever was behind it came into the room. The small she-wolf carried a tray with three plates filled with food. Another she-wolf followed her with glasses and a pitcher of what looked like tea. Axel's and Lucas's scent wafted in with the omegas, letting me know that they were out there, ready for whatever might happen in this room.

"Let's take a break from these talks." My father sat down at his desk, and the other alpha sat opposite him. The omega's sat two plates in front of the two alphas. "Nolen, come grab you a plate."

I stood from the chair, went up to the brunette she-wolf, and she handed me a plate, the taller female poured me a glass of tea. I took my food and tea over to the couch so that I would have room to spread out and eat. Setting the glass down on the maple coffee table, I started scooping mashed potatoes and green beans into my mouth. While my father and Alpha Wade sat at his desk, Wade continued to stare at me.

"So, you have two sons, Alpha Nero?" The old Alpha spoke, pointing to me with his fork. His hardened gaze glared at me; I never lowered my eyes. I knew it was a challenge, but I would never let anyone bully me again.

"Yes, had, Alpha Wade. Nolen is my youngest son. He will take over once his training is complete." My father smiled over at me and grinned back to him; before he realized he was glaring at me, his brows knitted in confusion.

"And when will you be through with your training, boy?"

My gaze went from my father to the older Alpha as I scooped up more food from my plate. "Whenever my father says I'm finished I suppose."

"Hmmm." Alpha Wade continued to eat his food, turning back to my father.

Alpha Wade had been here for seven days. He nor my father would concede anything, the alpha should have left, but he didn't. Sarge nagged at me in the back of my mind that the Dolostone alpha was up to something else, and I agreed with him. Between training and the meetings, I hadn't been to see Amora. I tried to sit in on all the discussions, but I still had training to do, and my father would not let me miss those.

Sparing with Axel, Lucas, and Daylen was the only way to make it fair. They all were older than me and more experienced, but they still had trouble taking me down. We continued to spar into the late morning, until we heard yelling from the packhouse. We each glanced at each other before we sprinted to the commotion.

Reaching the uproar, we discovered my father and Alpha Wade bellowing at each other on the steps. My father was so angry his face was red, and his wolf seemed to be trying to make his appearance as well. I ran to the top of the steps, Axel, Lucas, and Daylen following close behind. Alpha Wade glared over at me. I could tell his wolf was at the surface. He brandished his finger at me as I took my place beside my father. "You, boy! You better be on your guard! Otherwise, you will be dead just like your brother!"

"I don't take threats well! If you try to come back to this pack, I will make sure your bloodstains these steps just like my brother's," I warned, stepping forward away from my father in front of Alpha Wade. My voice was controlled yet threatening, I had been bullied far too long to step aside and let some other alpha bully me on my own pack lands.

"If you think this threat will be taken seriously, you are sadly mistaken!"

"Too bad. It's not a threat but a promise," I voiced; I could sense Sarge at the surface, pushing to get out. Alpha Wade glared at me before I noticed his gaze go past me for a fraction of a second. He turned away from my father and me and strolled down the steps into his vehicle.

CHAPTER THIRTEEN: THREE HUNDRED AND FIFTY DAYS

AMORA

The past two years flew by; I turned seventeen a few days ago. Nolen had not been able to come to this one, which made me a little sad. He did send his gift, though, and oh my Goddess was it perfect! Inside a small rectangular box was a small tennis bracelet.

Sawyer nor my parents didn't seem to be surprised by the gift. Making me a little skeptical that it had come from Nolen until I read his small note inside; I could recognize his writing anywhere. My brother even offered to help me put it on. I was a little shocked by this since he would go into a fit of rage most of the time if any male came up to me to ask me out.

"It's beautiful, Amora!"

"Who did it come from! This is so expensive!"

I smiled at the dainty bracelet on my wrist before glancing up at Sarah and Destini. "Would you believe it came from Nolen?"

They stopped and stared back at me, their mouths hanging open. "What!"

"Is he your mate?!"

"No, he didn't claim me when he turned eighteen. But he's like a brother, so I figure... Ya know?" I stared at the bracelet, smiling at it. They both continued to stare at me. I rolled my eyes at them and started making my way to the table that held all the food. I began to make a plate, but each time the door opened, I glanced over to see if Nolen had made it but was disappointed each time. Grabbing a bottle of water, I went to sit down, Sarah and Destini catching back up with me before I got to my table.

"He must be wanting you as a chosen mate then. A bracelet like this is more than a brother thing." Destini sat in the chair in front of me; she was always the direct one, never missing a beat to tell someone what was on her mind. Sarah took a seat beside me with her plate, gazing between Destini and me.

"He wouldn't do that. He knows I'd wait on my mate." Chewing on my lip, I scooped up food. This was not entirely true. If Nolen would ask me, I'd say yes, a million times over and never think twice about it. I fantasized about him sweeping me off my feet and making me his. If only he was my mate or would choose me.

Both girls nodded while giving me mischievous grins.

)))) 🐺 (((((

It had been two weeks since my seventeenth birthday, and I sat at my desk writing in my diary my mother had given me when Danika walked into my open bedroom door. She came up to my window the left of my desk and stared out of it. "So, are you going to Nolen's Alpha ceremony?"

Continuing to write in the diary, the tennis bracelet laying delicately on my wrist as my hand dashed along the antique pages of the book with the calligraphy pen that Sawyer had given me. Glancing over at her from the corner of my eye, I answered, "Of course. It's tomorrow, is it not?"

"Yes, so we should be leaving today."

I glanced up fully at her as she stood by the window, her arms crossed under her breasts. Danika gazed down at me with a smile, stepping behind me and playing with my hair. She would be an excellent Luna to the pack; she had changed Sawyer just enough to make him a little more responsible. I closed the diary and stood up from my chair. A bag sat on my bed; I had packed a few clothes and added the book in my hand. "Will there be other packs at his ceremony?"

Danika nodded with a smile and grabbed the wrist that wore the bracelet, fingering it, her gaze coming back to mine. "This was such a wonderful gift, and yes, there will be."

"Then there will be more opportunities for Nolen to find his mate." I pulled my hand from hers while mumbling as I finished packing my bag. I turned with my bag on my shoulder to Danika. "How soon are we leaving?"

"Pretty soon. Go ahead downstairs. That way they can put your stuff in the vehicle." Danika moved to me, placing a hand on my shoulder. Nodding, I proceed out of my room and down the stairs. I put my bag with the others and went into the living room where my mother, father, and Sawyer were, along with Beta Adam and Delta Eric; they all appeared to be in a heated discussion. They kept their voices where I could barely make out what they were saying, and when I walked in, they all immediately stopped talking.

Crossing my arms, I tilted my head, giving them all a curious gaze. They all had been acting strange around me since Nolen had shifted and we'd arrived back home. "Are you all having a secret meeting? Normally those are done in your office, father."

My father gave me a grin and Sawyer stepped forward, a smile forming on his face. "Why do you always suspect people? Huh?"

"Well, when people are in a room speaking low and then someone comes in and they all become quiet, I feel like that is something to suspect people of," I countered as he stood before me, the smile still playing on his face. I swear I believed he thought he was the best secret keeper, when really he wasn't, because as kids he would always cave and end up telling me. So, I felt confident he would eventually let whatever they were talking about slip.

Sawyer laughed as he strolled past me, patting me on the shoulder as he continued through the doors of the packhouse. Sighing, I went over to my mother. She pulled me into a hug and smiled. "The vehicles should be here soon, and we will be leaving. Do you have everything you need for the next two days?"

"Yes, Mother."

A warrior came into the room and bared his neck to us before standing up straight. He glanced over to my father and then my mother before his gaze landed on me. He quickly glanced back to my father as he stood in the doorway. "The vehicles are here. We are loading the baggage as we speak."

"Thank you very much. We will be out shortly." My father nodded to the warrior and motioned for Beta Adam and Delta Eric to follow him. The way the beta and delta gazed at me still made me curious about what they'd all been discussing when I came into the room.

My mother and I went out of the packhouse and to the cars, getting into the middle vehicle and waiting for the others to join us.

We were about five miles away from the Rhyolite pack territory when we suddenly stopped. I glanced between my brother and Danika, then at my mother and father. Sawyer pulled out his phone, dialing someone. My father got out of the vehicle just as Beta Adam got out of the front seat. Glancing out the side windows, I noticed that wolves were surrounding us.

Sawyer spoke into the phone with a worried tone, "Hey, man. Did you send a greeting party? No? Okay, well, we may end up needing help. Alright, let me know when you all get here. She's okay, alright, see you soon."

I stared at Sawyer; his face emotionless as he slowly shook his head. I sat back in my seat and took hold of my mother's hand. Sawyer opened the door to the SUV and stepped out. He shut the door with a quick snap, and I fixed my eyes on my brother as he strolled up to our dad and Beta Adam.

None of the wolves that encircled us moved other than to lick their jowls, keeping their drool from the ground. I stared outside of the SUV; my father and brother were too still, the air tense as all the wolves held their ground. Something was happening, the tension in the air was unbearable, and everything was way too calm.

A quick bark with a howl sounded out. I glanced over at my mother, whose face paled. Sawyer, my dad, and Beta Adam never moved a muscle, but the wolves seemed a little on edge since the sound. Snarls and growls resounded from my left. Which prompted my brother, father, and the beta to shift, bounding after the wolves in front of them.

Danika, my mother, and I sat in the SUV, waiting for the fighting to end. Wolves crashed into one another, sinking their teeth into the other. Blood splattered the left side of the vehicle and I turned to see a massive black and grey wolf with golden eyes standing beside our vehicle. It shook his head, flinging blood on everything that was close.

"Nolen." My heart started to race as he gazed at me. With a wink, Nolen ran off into the fray of fur and claws on the other side of the motorcade, tearing apart wolves and helping out my brother, father, and the beta. He was amazing to watch, even though it was a little gory.

I let go of my mother and pressed myself up against the SUV's window. The last of the wolves that surrounded us ran off. My father, brother, and the beta returned in wolf form along with Nolen in his. "Sawyer says they will run back with Nolen alongside the vehicles." Danika glanced between my mother and me. Nolen must have been the one Sawyer had called, and he came to help us out. If I had my wolf and had been his mate, I could have mind linked with him like the other wolves. I couldn't take my eyes off his magnificent wolf as he ran on my side of the vehicle.

Nolen

When we arrived back at the packhouse, the girls went in and the others came and got their things. Sawyer, Alpha Roman, and I, along with the warriors that had shifted to take down the pack of wolves, stayed in wolf form, watching as others took the SUVs to be washed.

It's a good thing Sawyer called us. Sarge shook his large head as Sawyer's wolf came up and nudged us. We followed him to around the back of the packhouse and shifted into human form.

Yes, it was a good thing he did. Turning to Sawyer, the blood that had stuck to our fur now stained our skin. Sawyer grinned at me as he came up to me, pulling me into a bloody hug. "Thanks for having our back. I don't think we would've had anyone left if you didn't."

"You know I would come to help you in a heartbeat, and not just because of her. You are practically my brother now," I told him as we went up the pack steps. Alpha Roman and Beta Adam had gone ahead of us to the shower room. I turned to the wolves that had yet to turn back, motioning for them to follow us. "Come on. You deserve a shower. There's plenty of room, so shift and come get cleaned up."

Sawyer and I went through the back doors of the building and into the shower room, which used to give me anxiety. Members of my pack had bullied me in here, and this is where Archer had first caught them. He had been livid that afternoon after he had just finished with training to find me being bullied in the showers. I thought he would tear the place apart.

My father had this renovated when I was training with Sawyer and his pack. It had new tile and faucets, and lockers lined the wall separating the front room and the showers. Alpha Roman and Beta Adam came out just as Sawyer and I grabbed towels and a bar of soap.

"Hurry up, boys. We still have dinner to get to, and you know how your mother is, Nolen." Alpha Roman strolled by a towel wrapped around his waist. For a man in his sixties, he was still very fit.

"We won't be long, Alpha Roman. There are clothes here for you to wear if you need them," I said, pointing over to the cabinets that held extra clothes in them. Sawyer and I stepped into a cubical and turned on the warm water, cleaning the blood and sweat off our bodies. I switched off the water and pulled a towel off the bar, drying the droplets away from my skin. Wrapping the towel around my waist, I walked out of the shower room and back into the first room.

Opening the cabinets, I pulled out a pair of shorts to put on, letting me head to my room so that I could dress for dinner. Looking behind me, Sawyer must have had the same idea since he had just a pair of shorts on as well. We both left the showers and headed up to the rooms above.

Everyone was heading into the dining room. The un-mated she-wolves snickered and flirted with me as they entered the hall. Sawyer cocked an eyebrow at me, and I shook my head at him as we went up the stairs. "I don't pay them any mind. They still won't give up, and they try to persuade me to take one of them as a chosen mate."

"Yeah, I'm glad my mate was near and of age. Otherwise, I'd be in the same boat as you." Sawyer stopped at the door he had stayed in the last time he and his family had come. He looked over my shoulder, nodding to the door on the other side of the room next to mine. "You realize she chose that one, right?"

Glancing over my shoulder, I smiled and then turned back to him. "I'm glad she kept the room. Her scent has been all but gone for a while now."

The door behind me opened, and her sweet scent invaded my senses. Sarge pushed himself up to the surface as I gazed at Sawyer before I turned around to face Amora as she stood there, letting her eyes roam over me. When our eyes met, she grinned at me, wetting her lips with her tongue. "Hey, Nolen."

"Hey, Amora. I'm sorry I wasn't able to make it to your birthday. Did you receive your present?" I held my ground, trying to avoid grabbing her up and taking her into my room. Glancing down at her wrist, I saw the small bracelet resting lightly on it.

"Of course, I love it. I understand. I'm sure you had some pack business that needed to be taken care of." One of her hands went to her hair, twirling a light brown strand around her finger.

"I was busy. But I tried to make it, I really did." Sarge had pushed so far up that my voice sounded more animalistic, while I tried to keep him back. He made this more complicated as he fought me, even though he knew we couldn't have her yet.

Amora strode to me, and I locked my muscles as she neared. Her hand reached out to touch my bare skin, and I watched every movement as her skin found mine. Amora's fingers softly traced my torso before she pulled her hand away. The way her skin ignited mine told me that the bond was getting stronger, and she could sense it more since she was closer to her eighteenth birthday.

She glanced up at me, surprise in her eyes before she turned her gaze to Sawyer behind me. Sawyer's hand landed on my shoulder, reminding me that I needed to take back control of myself and Sarge. *Bud, you need to chill out. She still needs time.*

I know, but her being so near when we have been so far away… Sarge started to rescind back into my mind, his sadness coming through my emotions.

Sarge, we only have to wait three hundred and fifty more days. I gazed at her, taking in every bit of her beauty. That beautiful mouth and her gorgeous amber eyes held mine as she again wet her lips with her tongue.

Only three hundred and fifty more days, and you will be mine.

CHAPTER FOURTEEN: ALPHA CEREMONY

After helping Sawyer and his group arrive safely in the territory, I told my dad to send out a few warriors to help make sure the other packs were not ambushed as well. But they made it in without a problem, which made me think they were after the Quartzite pack.

But what would they want from them? Could it be because we have an alliance with them? I wondered, pacing my bedroom after dinner because sleep would not come to me. Amora slept in the next room, and I heard her soft breaths through the walls. Her scent calmed me and excited me at the same time.

They could have been after Amora. Sarge laid down in my head, his ears laid back flat.

But why? That had been another reason I hadn't said she was ours. No one would realize she was our mate. I ran my hand down my face and then back through my hair. This whole thing was ridiculous. I mean, they had to know she was our mate. But who would have told? I'd only told Sawyer, mom, and dad. Unless someone had been eavesdropping on the conversation.

Dinner had been entertaining with all the packs under one roof. My father had invited most of the packs to my Alpha ceremony tomorrow. Many of them had brought their daughters to see if they were my mate, hoping to bridge an alliance with my pack and, therefore, Sawyer's.

Amora had sat beside Danika as I'd sat beside my father and Sawyer. The other Alphas and their Lunas sat at different tables, talking, and laughing. This was how we should be—friends and alliances coming together to be as one. But once tomorrow ended, only some would still be alliances. Others would go on as if they had not broken bread with the wolves they now sat beside.

I needed to sleep, but all these questions and thoughts kept me awake. Closing my eyes, I rested my hands on the top of my head. I took a deep breath, trying to make myself tired. I had not even taken over the title of Alpha, and yet I couldn't figure out why the Quartzite pack had been attacked.

"Nolen, can you not sleep?"

I turned quickly to face Amora. She stood in the doorway connecting her room to mine. My side of the door had not been locked, and I had no intention of doing so, because if she wanted to come to me, then she should be able to without having to go into the hall. Her cami and shorts hugged her body as if it was a second layer of skin.

"No. I've been thinking of things." My eyes continued to wander over her body; her hair had just a little bit of mess to it. I wondered if she couldn't sleep either, this was the second time she'd opened the door.

"Anything I can help with?" She placed her hands on her hips, swaying them to one side. Damn, just that slight movement of her body and she had me wanting her even more.

"No. Nothing to worry yourself about," I assured, smiling over at her, excited that she had wandered into my room. I must have been making more noise than I thought.

"Are you worried about tomorrow when you take over the pack?" Amora stepped forward into my room, and when she reached me, she placed her hands on my bare chest. The fire and sparks her touch ignited ran through my body. She traced my tattoo with her hand along with her eyes. I tried to keep my breath and heart rate steady, but that was always futile when she was around.

"Not really. Why are you awake?" I grabbed her hand to stop her from tracing further down, her eyes anchoring themselves to mine. Those amber orbs stole my soul.

"I couldn't sleep. My mind has been wandering for days." She pressed her body flush against mine, her other hand slipped around to my back. "Nolen."

"Amora, what are you doing?" I tightened my grip on her hand resting on my chest. Her heartbeat faster beneath her breast, I could smell her arousal. *She's experiencing the bond more. She wants us, Nolen.* "I thought you wanted to wait for your mate."

"I do, but there are days when I would give him up for you, and I don't understand why." Amora's eyes searched and pleaded with mine to tell her the answer to her statement, an answer I could not reveal to her just yet. Even though I wanted to with all my heart.

I caressed her cheek with the tips of my fingers, her skin soft under my calloused fingers, she leaned her head into my hand, her eyes fluttering closed before opening again to gaze back into mine. "I don't know how to answer you. Tell me what you are feeling, Amora."

"At this moment?"

I nodded to her as I pulled her closer to me.

"I feel this lure, this attraction to you and only you. I can be around any other male and not experience this, but I come within yards of you, and I can't help but think about your scent. Your hands touching me like they are now, your lips on mine."

My heart raced in its cage as she turned from me. Anxiety drove me forward as I grabbed her hand, twisted her back around, and pulled her back to me. "Don't be joking with me, Amora. Do you want me to kiss you?"

Amora nodded, wetting her lips with her tongue. I caged her body to me, one arm around her waist and then the other at the back of her head. I took her mouth with mine. My lips punished hers as her hands landed on my chest, making this all the more intense as we melded into one another's embrace. At this moment, we were as one as we could be. She nipped my bottom lip, and I felt her tongue slip in against mine. *I wish she was of age; she tastes so sweet,* Sarge panted in my head as I continued to kiss Amora. She moaned against my lips, and it left a tingling sensation on them, making me groan into our kiss.

This was becoming more heated than I had wanted to go, I could feel myself hardening, and there was no possible way she didn't notice it pressing into her stomach. I broke our kiss to try to douse the burning before it went too far. Amora sighed; her hand went to her lips, and she traced her fingertips over her swollen mouth. "That was amazing. Have you kissed many girls before?"

Chuckling, I cupped her face, keeping her eyes on me. I shook my head; her hands ran down my torso to my hips. *Why don't you kiss her again, Nolen?* "You should know that answer, Amora."

"Even when you lived at my pack?"

"No."

Amora smiled, tightening her grip on my hips. Her eyes flirted with me as she gazed up at me. This woman could tell me to jump off a cliff and I would do it just to make her happy.

"Can I kiss you again?" I realized I sounded desperate, but she had allowed me to kiss her for the first time, and now I wanted to kiss her all night if she would let me.

"Please!"

I didn't think twice before crashing my lips back on hers.

A sharp rap on my door yanked me from my slumber. I sat up, glancing around the room, trying to get my bearings. The door to Amora's room stood wide open, and I glanced beside me. My heart skipped a beat when I saw her in my bed under the covers. The knock came again, and the person on the other side tried to open the door. The knob jiggled, and I was glad that it was reinforced with Tungsten rods.

Good thing I made you lock that last night. Sarge swept his tail from side to side as he laid down in my mind as if he was as content as a fish in a bowl.

I lifted the covers to ensure that her clothes remained on her body, and to my satisfaction, they were. She was still a minor, even though she was my mate. I was sure I would be reprimanded for anything that happened to her.

"Nolen! Open the door, man. You need to be getting ready! You've slept almost all day." Sawyer's voice sounded muffled behind the door. My brain went into overdrive as I tried to figure out how to move Amora out of my bed. There was no way he didn't realize she was in my room.

"Yeah! I'm getting up. Be out in a minute." Sawyer's footsteps faded away, and, luckily, he didn't go to Amora's room.

I turned to Amora's sleeping form beside me and shook her softly. Her eyes fluttered open, and I heard her heart start to race in panic. "Hey, it's okay. Nothing happened."

She did the same thing I did and lifted the covers from her body before she started to calm back down. "Oh, my Goddess, Nolen. I'm so sorry, I shouldn't have come to you. I don't know what made me act like that! And we kissed, Nolen." Her hand went up to her mouth as she stared at me, her eyes as big as saucers.

"I don't regret the kiss, do you?" I started to think I should have refused her and told her to go back to her room.*I'm glad you didn't.*"I asked you if you wanted me to kiss you, you said yes."

"I don't regret it. But how did we end up in bed together?" She lowered her gaze to her hands, which were resting in her lap. Her messy hair hid her face from my gaze.

*You both were pretty passionate about the kissing. I'm surprised you're both are alive. I didn't know if you were going to come up to breathe.*I grabbed her chin, making her look back at me; she seemed about to cry. "I don't remember laying down with you. But you are still clothed, and so am I. Nothing happened, and I wouldn't disrespect you like that."

Amora lunged into me, hugging me from the side. I pulled her into my lap so that both of us would be more comfortable. She didn't try to stop me and tightened her grip around my neck. I rubbed her back as we sat there on my bed. Amora sat back on my legs and gazed into my eyes. "So, I was your first kiss?"

"Was I that bad?"

"No, it's just I didn't ever think I would be someone's first kiss. I mean, I don't know." Her eyes searched mine, and I didn't want to leave this room. I wanted to stay right here until she could recognize the bond.

"Well, if you don't want to get caught in my bed by your brother, I suggest you head to your room. He has already been banging on my door. We slept for a while, and the ceremony will be starting soon," I told her as I tucked a lock of her hair behind her ears.

"Really! I need time to get ready!" Amora jumped off me and raced into her room. She forgot to close the door, and I laughed at her as I got up. I leaned against the door frame, watching her dig through her bag, pulling out an outfit, bra, and panties. Amora grabbed up all her clothes and headed into the bathroom to change.

I turned away from the open entrance and went over to my walk-in closet, where I took a collared shirt, dress pants, and a vest from the hangers. Putting everything on, I exited the small room and opened the top drawer of my dresser, grabbing socks so that I could put on my shoes. Sitting down on my bed, I slipped on my socks and dress shoes.

When I glanced over to the open doorway, a smile grew on my face. Amora had on a tight-fitting black dress and high heels. She sat at the vanity, fixing up her hair and starting on her make-up. "Hey, not too much, okay?"

She glanced over at me and snickered before staring back at herself in the mirror. I liked her without too much make-up, and no make-up at all.

Amora stood up and admired herself in the mirror then turned to me. "You want to walk down with me? Or do you think people would talk?"

Amora smiled and then sauntered up to me, readjusting my vest a bit before glancing up to me. "Do you think they will talk?"

"I could care less if they do. I just don't want you getting hurt." I ran my thumb across her cheek, tilting her head up to me.

"Nolen, with you by my side, no one will hurt me. And besides, I'm not a damsel in distress." She winked at me before she placed a chaste kiss on my lips.

Smirking at her, I took a deep breath of her before I laid my cheek next to hers as I whispered, "You kissed me that time. Are we going to be kissing friends?"

"I'll never tell." She wove her arm with mine, giving me a mischievous glance, and I opened the door.

I overheard everyone downstairs milling about, waiting for me to arrive at the hall where the stage sat. Axel and Lucas were pacing the bottom of the stairs until they glanced up and saw Amora and me descending the stairs.

"Damn, man, how long can you sleep? The alpha was about to come up there to throw you out of bed." Lucas's gaze went from me to Amora and then back again with a not-too-subtle wink.

Huffing, I rolled my eyes as Axel shrugged and then started ahead of us. I motioned for the red-headed wolf to follow him since they both would be up on stage with me. He finally took the hint and followed Axel, and I glanced over to Amora before going after them. "You okay with walking with me to the stage? You realize all those un-mated she-wolves may press you."

"I'm not afraid of them, Nolen. If you remember, I'm of alpha blood as well."

"Touché." We strolled into the room, and everyone stared at us as we headed to the stage. My father and mother gave me a curious look, Danika's mouth was hanging open at the sight of us, but Sawyer looked like he would jump into the air. When we got up to the stage, I turned to Amora and kissed her hand before she went over to her family. I stayed with my mom as my dad walked up to the front of the stage.

"Now that my son decided to grace us with his appearance. We can proceed with the ceremony!" He raised his arms, silencing the chuckling that resounded through the crowd. "Tonight, Nolen will take over the Alpha title, and while he has yet to find his Luna, we're certain that she will be found soon. Without further ado, we will start the ceremony."

I glanced over my shoulder at Amora and winked at her. She grinned and leaned into Danika's ear and said something to her. Turning back around, I faced the pack that I would be leading. One of the elders walked by me to my father with the ceremonial dagger. Stepping forward where the elder stood between us, I observed the crowd. My heart was racing; I had never been good at being in front of a group of people.

"Rhyolite pack! From this moment forward, you will be under a new leader. Under this new moon, we will bring a new Alpha to lead the pack." The elder's voice was loud and strong for being as old as he was. He continued with the ceremonial words, and I tuned him out until he grabbed hold of my left wrist and slit my palm, along with my father's. He placed them both together and started chanting; I sensed the power course through our hands as the leadership passed from my father to me. It took all my strength and Sarge's to keep us standing as the power started to ebb.

I pulled my hand away, and at that moment, I felt stronger than I had ever experienced. Sarge was at the surface, trying to come free, and instead of holding him back, I let him out. Within seconds the large black and grey wolf stood in my spot, Sarge's mind became sharper, and when he looked out over the pack, they all knelt and bared their necks to him.

CHAPTER FIFTEEN: ALPHA NOLEN

My father stayed by me to help when I needed him to. Axel joined the ranks that night too. He was with me in every meeting and helped with keeping chaos down, since a few of the wolves who'd bullied me didn't think I should be Alpha without my mate. It's not like I didn't want her; I just couldn't claim her at this moment.

I ended up telling Axel, Lucas, and Daylen about Amora. Which seemed to put them all three at ease. At which point they decided to tease me about her, and I realized they were trying to make me feel included.

I found out Axel had found his mate from one of the other packs, and she'd stayed behind to be with him. Daylen found his as well; she was a little shy at first, especially with me since I was now Alpha, but it didn't take her long to realize I was not like the others she had been around.

Sitting at my father's desk—well, mine, I went through the financial paperwork. My father kept them very well managed. We always maintained room to do what needed to be done without going above our means.

Rhyolite was a large pack, and with it being as sizable as it was, it meant other packs who happened to not be our allies wanted to overthrow us. One was Alpha Wade and the Dolostone pack, who continued to make threats, and my warriors and I continued to push back the threats they tried to make good on.

Yesterday had been one such attack, but we'd pushed them back with little force. I felt like they persisted in trying to find our weak spots, but they had not been able to break past. Axel and Lucas thought the same; we doubled our patrols to keep the rest of the pack safe.

Sawyer had not been attacked, and he kept me updated on how Amora was doing since I couldn't run off and sneak around to see her anymore. She started texting me more since we kissed, and it made me feel so much better that she would actually talk to me. Sawyer planned a massive party for her birthday.

I had already purchased my gifts for her, and I was excited to be there when she shifted. *Once she was ours, we would be stronger, and then we could take Alpha Wade.* Sarge sat on his haunches, his tail sweeping the floor.

The long wait would be over in a couple of weeks, and she would be by my side for the rest of my life. Figuring out how to get Alpha Wade to stop attacking us happened to prove challenging. My warriors began to train harder for the looming battle. My pack drilled twice as hard now that the threats were more frequent. My father had decided he needed to be involved with the pack, so he'd become one of the trainers.

Sir! We have Dolostone wolves at the gate. Alpha Wade is here as well! One of the patrol wolves' mind linked me urgently. I stood up from my desk while Sarge snarled in my head. These wolves were relentless in their pursuit of my pack.

I'm on my way. I opened the doors to my office and stripped as I shifted into Sarge. *This Alpha thinks he can just show up unannounced; I will rip his head from his shoulders!* We made it to the gate, where wolves and humans snarled and yelled at each other.

Shifting back to my human form, I waded through the crowd. My pack hushed as I passed them, I knew being naked got their attention, but the aura I now possessed did as well. Alpha Wade sneered at me as I stepped in front of him. I crossed my arms over my chest; Axel and Lucas stood on either side of me in wolf form, fangs showing in silent snarls. "Alpha Wade, is there a reason you are here at my gate with a battalion of warriors?"

"I'm here to take your territory and pack. Concede now, or there will be no more of your line." Alpha Wade took a step closer to me; the two wolves beside me gave him a warning growl, one even snapped at his feet, his eyes shot over to them, but they held their ground.

"That won't happen. I will not hand my territory and pack over just like that. You might be able to convince other alphas to do that, but you won't obtain mine without a fight." Approving howls and voices rose behind me as I continued to glare at Alpha Wade.

"That's fine. I will take your pack and territory by force. I wouldn't sleep too hard at night." He turned to walk away from me. His wolves still growling and snapping at mine, I wouldn't let him slaughter my pack in their sleep. Pups would not be afraid to go to sleep at night.

"No, we will end this with an Alpha challenge. No other wolves will be hurt. We fight now, or you leave and never set foot back on my territory again." Alpha Wade stopped in his tracks before he turned to me, his eyes the color of his wolf's as a sadistic grin played on his face.

))))◗🐺◖(((((

Amora

The more people talked about the prophecy and started to compare it with Nolen and his family, I finally decided to do some research for myself. I made my way to the library archives in the older part of the packhouse. Sawyer had mentioned it to me, and then I'd heard whispers about it from the pack.

I loved coming to the library; the smell of the books put me more at ease than anything. Well, almost anything, Nolen definitely was number one now. I was excited since my eighteenth birthday was two weeks away. Finding out who my mate would be scared me as well; what if it wasn't Nolen?

Shaking my head, I turned my attention to the task at hand. I went further back into the catacombs of books until I found the shelf I had been searching for. Ambling down the aisle, I came to the section I needed and pulled up a step stool. Climbing it, I peered at the titles before finding the one I thought would help me.

Taking the book to the closest table, I opened it to start my hunt for answers. Reading through the pages of this book gave me no more insight than what I had heard in town.

Two siblings' destinies intertwine. Both unmated. One must lose while the other shall die to restore the balance and fuel the destiny written in the stars. Only then can man and wolf be with their one true mate.

What could this mean? It could be Nolen and Archer. His brother died seven years ago, but how would Nolen lose? How did their destinies intertwine?

Snapping the book shut, I replaced it back where I found it. Then there was the dream I had when Nolen shifted for the first time, running to someone and then another laughing cruelly as the person I ran to sprinted away from me.

This was all so confusing; I strolled blindly through the halls; one thing on my mind, I wanted it to be my birthday now. That way, I could deter-mine if my feelings for Nolen were the mate bond or something else. If they were not the mate bond, I don't know what I would do; I felt like my heart would break. But then it would mean these feelings were not real, that I had made myself fall for this other alpha heir that would not reciprocate my feelings.

"Hey, sis! You going to ignore me?" Glancing up, I saw Sawyer at the door to his office. Dad had finally stepped down and let him become Alpha, and Danika became Luna. I grinned at my brother, making my way to him. Dad and mom had decided to take a trip abroad and would be back a week before my birthday.

"Hey, sorry, I was in my own little world." I gave him a hug. I still did things that I really shouldn't, but hey, that was me.

"I could see that. What are you racking your mind about now?" Sawyer folded his arms over his chest and leaned against the door frame. He had been keeping an extra close eye on me since Nolen's Alpha ceremony. I often wondered if he knew I had been in Nolen's bed.

"I don't know, a lot will change in two weeks, and I'm not entirely sure how I will feel about certain things." I shrugged as I glanced around at the omegas cleaning the hall.

"You've been sitting in with mom and Danika, right? Learning as much as you can about pack things?" Peering back at him, I gave him a questionable look, while his face remained expressionless. This was another reason I was confused. Why make me sit in these types of things? Did someone know something I didn't?

"Yeah, I mean, Mom is very adamant that I do. I'd rather be training with Beta Adam, but those are few and far between now."

"You have to have a little of everything. What if you are a mate to an Alpha? You need to figure out what to do and how to handle the pack." He pushed himself off the door frame and placed his arm around my shoulders, leading me away from his office. "By the way, I know you have been talking to Nolen. What is our brother from another pack doing nowadays?"

"You talk with him too. Maybe even more than I do. Why are you asking?" I asked, stopping in my tracks to stare at him. He knew something, and he wasn't telling me. Nolen and I had been talking more since I left this time, which had me over the moon because I missed him.

"Yeah, well, I figured he would have different stuff to talk to you about. I mean, you are like a sister to him." He continued forward, laughing. Rolling my eyes, I caught back up to him, slapped him on the back of the head, and ran for it.

I knew I would not stay ahead of him long since he had his wolf and I still didn't. He caught back up to me within seconds and grabbed me from behind. Twisting me around to face him. "Why in the hell would you slap me?"

"I don't know, it seemed like a good idea at the moment," I told him as we walked back to the packhouse. He wasn't angry with me. I used to do this to him all the time when we were kids, and so what if he was Alpha now.

"So, what are you hoping to get on your birthday?"

"Nothing. Just ready to find out who my mate will be." I peered over at him from the corner of my eye, his lips pursed like he was deep in thought. He glanced back at me, a smile playing on his lips. That smile meant he was up to no good. Even though he'd become Alpha, he was still my brother, and I knew him like the back of my hand.

"I believe he will be strong, sorta on the good-looking side, but not as good-looking as me. Besides, he's gonna have to be patient to deal with your shenanigans." He puffed his chest up and started strutting around ahead of me. I couldn't help but bust out laughing. This brother of mine drove me bat shit crazy, but other times he made me laugh when I wanted to cry. If I did have a mate in another pack, I would miss him.

I ran up to Sawyer and hugged him tightly. "I love you to the farthest moon and back, big brother!"

"I love you too, little sis. And believe me, if your mate ever mistreated you, I would go to war for you." Sawyer pulled me tight against him. We didn't always get along, but these were the times I cherished. "Come on, let's go have dinner."

We made our way to the packhouse and into the dining room. Danika was sitting at the alpha table along with Beta Adam and Delta Eric on the other side of Sawyer's chair. I took my seat next to Danika on her right side. Sawyer had yet to name a new beta and delta since Beta Adam's daughter was still just a kid and Delta Eric's daughter was now the Luna.

Other wolves made their way in, and I noticed some of them were part of the trainees that Sawyer and Nolen had trained with. They were now with the patrols, making sure that the territory was protected. That is when another male stumbled through the crowd, pushing his way up to Sawyer. The unknown male fell before he made it to Sawyer; my brother stood and ran from his seat over to the male, pulling him to a sitting position against the table. "Who are you? Why did you come?"

"Alpha. Rhyolite... Alpha Nolen... Alpha Wade beat him. He is believed dead, Alpha."

CHAPTER SIXTEEN: ROGUE

My breath hitched at the male's words, and when my brother glanced over to me, I could see it in his face what my mind was trying to tell me. My hands went to my mouth as the sob escaped from me; I shook my head, the tears bubbled up in my eyes. This was not true! He couldn't be dead! I had just spoken to him this morning. "Sawyer, send a scout to find out what happened! We need to know!"

"I realize that, Amora!" he snapped at me before he ran his hand down his face. He gave me a sorrowful glance before he turned to survey the room around him. "I need two wolves to go to the Rhyolite pack to see what has happened."

The whole room of wolves stepped forward; Sawyer picked out two wolves. So distraught with the grief of possibly having lost Nolen, I couldn't understand what was happening as Luna Danika pulled me close to her and then swept me away to my room.

I sobbed on my bed; Danika sat beside me, rubbing my back. Why would the Goddess do this to me? Why would she give me these feelings and take the wolf those feelings burned for away? Danika continued to rub my back until I blacked out from exhaustion.

$$ \text{)} \text{)} \text{)} \text{)} \text{)} \text{)} \text{ 🐺 } \text{(} \text{(} \text{(} \text{(} \text{(} \text{(} $$

The wolves that Sawyer sent came back, but not with news that we wanted to hear. He was not there leading his pack. Nolen's father and mother were in the dungeons, put there by Alpha Wade.

The pack was a skeleton of itself. None of the wolves made a sound; they worked and then went home. No one talked with each other. The two wolves couldn't get closer to the inner parts since Dolostone wolves patrolled the inside of the territory, keeping wolves away from the packhouse.

They told us the scent of blood flooded throughout the territory, and the crimson liquid seeped into the ground as bodies decayed becoming food for other scavengers while their families mourned them from afar. The settlement had become a wasteland.

My birthday was not what I imagined it. Oh, lots of wolves were at the celebration, along with unmated males that vied for my attention. But not the one I wanted vying for it. To me, it was a dull affair, and I didn't stay long, much to the displeasure of my mother and father.

I couldn't handle it; I didn't want to be near anyone. At least not who were present in the packhouse. The one I wanted at the party and who would have made it the most wonderful birthday in my life was possibly dead.

I ran away from the party and the people with it. Sprinting away to the woods, I started to feel snapping in my bones, and I whimpered, making it to the clearing where I first smelled his scent after he left.

Letting go of my grief and pain, I screamed out, allowing the wolves patrolling and any others know I was there. My gaze went to the sky. The flower moon shone tonight as I fell to the ground, my bones starting to reshape into my wolf. We both lay on the ground in her form, not knowing what we looked like.

Sleep, sweet one. You have had a very trying couple of weeks. Lie here and take in this wonderful scent. I will be with you from now till the end.

Nolen

Sarge limped through the forest, his head low to the ground. We lost, and not only did we lose our position, but we about lost our life. The old Alpha thought he had killed me. I lay still in the pool of blood as his wolf stepped away from me, and everyone left me for dead. Axel and Lucas tried to come to me, but the Dolostone wolves kept them back, pushing them back to the packhouse.

Now, I lingered in the back of Sarge's mind. I couldn't understand what happened during my fight with him, and then it changed so quickly. The pack would never want me as the Alpha again, I tried to protect them by issuing the Alpha challenge, but it didn't go the way I thought it would have.

Sarge came up to a creek and drank from the cool water. He had been silent, listening to the mantra of my thoughts since we were able to leave. Not knowing what to do or where to go. The Quartzite pack was the only other place I could think of, but if Alpha Wade realized I had not died, I'm sure he would go to their pack first.

We will have to stay rogue until we can become stronger and take back our pack, Sarge voiced as he glanced up to survey his surroundings.

I understand, but how do we become stronger? We trained with the best trainers, and yet he still somehow won.

I know. Sarge's ears drooped along with his tail.

We need to find a place to stay and heal some more, I told him.

He took off into the stream, belly deep in the water to hide our scent. I started to gaze at my surroundings, I didn't recognize any of this forest, but I had not really been paying attention to where Sarge had been taking us. He kept his guard up, his ears twisting and turning as he focused on what was before us.

We trotted through the stream for a few miles until we came to a beaver dam. Sarge jumped up on the embankment and went a few more miles through the woods until he came up to a massive tree. He started digging at the tree's roots until he fit himself into the hole.

I awoke the following morning hungry. Opening my eyes, I gazed out of Sarge's eyes which told me he was still in control. *You can take control back at any time, Nolen. I figured since we didn't have any clothes right now, you'd rather stay as me.*

Yes, that is a good point. I'd rather not be naked right now. But we do need to find some clothes. And food.

I can find our food easily. Sarge climbed out of the den he made; shaking the dirt from our fur, he stretched out our muscles before putting our nose to the sky. Sniffing for something to attract our senses.

We trotted forward into the woods, avoiding low-hanging branches in the trees and the twigs on the ground. A doe stood in a small clearing. She had not heard or detected us yet. We crouched in the bushes, ready to spring, when a fawn came out from the other side of the clearing. I stilled Sarge, *Let's find something else.* Sarge snorted, his ears against his head. *Then it will be longer before we eat.*

It's fine. I don't want to be the reason it loses its mother.

Moving from the brush, we pressed on, searching for food. Stopping by the stream, we drank our fill before continuing further into the woods. The feel of his strength as we padded away from the doe and the fawn still astounded me. *I could grow used to being you.*

A rabbit darted out, and Sarge ran after it. Pouncing on it, he took it into his strong jaws and broke its neck. He laid on the ground, tearing the flesh from its bones. The rabbit didn't take Sarge long to devour, but it was enough to help us go forward.

My brother and I used to come to hunt in the woods; well, he did; I just helped him. I miss him still. He would be ashamed of me right now. The thought of Archer gazing down on me right now and being disappointed in me for losing the pack.

No. Archer would not, Nolen. He would never be ashamed of you.

We continued searching for more food; I mean, we were larger than ordinary wolves, and the rabbit was just an appetizer. Happening upon a small encampment, Sarge circled it, sniffing around to find out if anyone resided at the moment in the camp. We cautiously moved forward into the campsite after determining that no one was around.

Nosing around in the tents and bags, we found some clothes. *Might be easier to make sure the clothes fit if we were human.*

We shifted, and I rifled through the clothes, grabbing two shirts, a pair of pants, and shorts. Grabbing a bag, I put the clothes and a few things of food. Shifting back, Sarge grabbed the bag with his muzzle, and we ran for the den he made beneath the tree.

It had been a few weeks since I'd encountered anyone. Amora still plagued my mind; would she wonder where I was? Be sad if I didn't return? I could never know. All I knew was that she was safe right now since my "death."

Sitting up against the tree that had become my home. I sat there thinking how I would be able to get my pack back without an army of wolves to fight with me. There was no way I would go to Sawyer and ask him to risk his when I was too weak to protect my own pack.

He would not want a weak alpha with his sister. Even if we were mates. Sarge whimpered in my head. Once we acquired clothes, I started being more human than wolf, we still had to hunt, and I let Sarge out to do that; he loved the thrill of it.

We will get our pack back, our birthright back, and save your parents.

I don't know if that will happen. I still have not figured out how to become stronger to defeat Alpha Wade. He's older. He should have been slower. Delta Eric told me this would happen.

What if this is part of our destiny? What if this was how we become strong? You keep telling yourself that you are not fit for being alpha, but that is not what your brother thought.

You never knew my brother or his thoughts.

Sarge was silent for some time. I thought he had ended the conversation, and I sat there looking out over the blooming forest. It was rather odd that I had not seen any other wolf in these woods. Not like I recognized what forest I lived in at the moment or what lived in it with me.

That's not true.

Before I could answer him, I heard snarls around me. Wolves surrounded me; I didn't know if they happened to be Dolostone wolves or a different pack. I sat there observing them, counting them. If I could not defeat one Alpha, how would I defeat the wolves in front of me?

You defeated two wolves when you were thirteen. You may have lost against that alpha, but you can still come back and take what is ours back.

And how do you think we will take back the pack when most of them didn't like me? Sawyer would never let Amora be by my side.

If you don't stand your stubborn, sulking ass up and protect yourself. I will make you.

I glanced around at the wolves who had not moved from their position. Standing, I started to shed my clothes, shifting within seconds. The wolves snarled and growled, showing their teeth to me. Sarge stood there snarling back, ears laid upon our head, challenging them to charge.

Some of them glanced at each other; one wolf crawled forward on his belly, showing me respect. He shifted while on the ground and knelt, baring his neck to us. He stared back up into our golden eyes with his green ones. "We have been waiting for you, Alpha Nolen."

CHAPTER SEVENTEEN: A NEW WAY

"What do you mean you were waiting for me? Hell, you came up to me about to tear me apart," I asked, glancing around at the now-shifted wolves after I had shifted back to my human form. They weren't familiar to me, which didn't mean much. Not everyone came to my Alpha ceremony.

The male who came up to me glanced up at me, then around to the other wolves in his company. "We didn't realize who you were till you shifted. The Goddess didn't inform us what you looked like in human form. We're sorry about the almost attack."

Goddess? Is this male for real?

I believe he is, Nolen.

"What do you mean, the Goddess?" I wasn't stupid; I understood who he was talking about, but no one I was friends with ever spoke with her, and yet this male said that he had talked with her.

The male gave me a concerned glance before he shook his head. "Boy, do you have some kind of condition? Or are you just plain stupid?"

"I'm not stupid, and I don't know who you are, but I will not be spoken to like that!" Sarge made his way to the surface, letting the older male understand he still outranked him. He gazed at me with a stoic expression, as if my rank meant little to him.

"You could've fooled me. Want to fill me in on why you are here and not with your pack?"

My heart sank to my stomach as I tore my eyes from him. This was still a sore subject, even though it had been weeks. "I lost an alpha challenge. Now I have to figure out how to get it back, if they still want me."

Nodding his head, he began to busy himself with building a fire. Glancing at him and the rest of the wolves, I fiddled with a stick I had found before throwing it into the now blazing flames. "So, will I learn your names anytime soon?"

The older wolf smiled at me, turning his gaze to mine. "My name's Olli. The others are Hannah, Fin, Markus, and Harley. We've all been summoned to help you."

"Help me what? There's no way the six of us can defeat the Dolostone pack." Doubt laced my voice. This wolf thought I was stupid, but he acted like we could take down the now biggest pack in the territory.

Olli laughed at me. Evidently, he thought I was funny, so I stood up and walked away. I wasn't about to start a fight I knew would end up killing me. But there was no way I could stay near that group of wolves while they laughed at me.

Ambling away from the weird pack of wolves, I started to notice footsteps. Rounding on the person behind me, I saw it was the wolf they called Fin. "What do you want? You come to laugh at me too?"

Fin crossed his arms while he stood there inspecting me. His hazel eyes never left me as we stared at each other. "Listen, I understand what you are going through. I lost my pack a long time ago, and then a few months ago, I was guided here to them. I don't know what the Goddess has in store for you, but I do know I'm here to make a difference for you, and so are they. You need help, and we are here to do that."

"And what are you and they going to teach me that I haven't already been taught?" I asked, glaring back at this male, waiting for his reply.

"We can teach you a lot and guide you to be able to obtain your pack back." Fin came up to me, face to face; he was just as big as I was. And the way he talked he must have been an Alpha as well. "You have too much strength to be letting this old Alpha take what is yours. It's time Alpha Wade is taken out before he decides he wants to be king over all of the werewolves."

"So, what are you all wanting me to do? Why would the Goddess care if I lost my pack? Alphas lose their packs all the time. What makes me special?"

"Have you heard the prophecy?"

"I've heard rumors of a prophecy. But I'm not unmated. I have a mate; she's just not old enough to feel the bond."

"Still unmated, my friend. You've not consummated the bond with her. So, she and you are still unmated. This prophecy may not be world-changing, or it might be. No one knows but the Moon Goddess herself. But I was instructed to come to this band of wolves to find you and help you along in your journey. If you are too proud to take help or want to wallow in self-pity, then I will take my leave right here." Fin glared at me, and I realized what he said was true.

That for the past few weeks, I had been too proud to ask for help, and I had made myself believe the pack didn't need me and Sawyer would keep Amora from me. Sawyer never once treated me like that, and deep down, I understood he would have my back as I would have his.

I glanced back to Fin and nodded. Even if it killed me, I would take back my pack and make Amora my Luna. "Fine, let's get started."

)))))🐺(((((

Training with the pack of wolves the Moon Goddess sent to me proved to be complicated. I learned that Fin had been an Alpha to a pack that long ago was ripped apart, and he, like myself, was kept alive and roamed the territories as a rogue. Until the Goddess came to him, telling him to find Olli.

Olli and Markus had been exiled by their previous Alpha for not condoning certain things. But they both taught me that no matter what, as long as you keep your emotions away during a fight, anyone can overcome anyone.

Hannah and Harley were twins, they were the youngest among us, but what they lacked in strength and knowledge, they made up in speed. They were almost as fast as an alpha, which stumped me. Their wolves even looked alike; the only way to tell them apart was they were male and female.

Between all of them, I started to learn more than what I had known before. Since they were rogue, after all, they taught me a completely different fighting style. Something I had never seen before, but I learned it, and I learned it well.

"You are learning fast, Nolen!" Hannah flipped out of my way as I tried to catch her to pin her, getting close each time but not being quick enough to grab her.

"Apparently not, since I still cannot catch you." I turned to keep her in my sight, which proved just as hard as keeping up with her.

"No one has ever caught me but my brother." She stayed just shy of my grasp, laughing as she did. "Anyway, I guess we can quit. It's about time for dinner."

I nodded and stretched out my muscles while we walked back to the cave we now resided in. The burning wood and cooking meat wafted over to us. Hannah skipped beside me as we went through the underbrush.

Entering the cave, the other four wolves glanced up before nodding to us and continuing with what they were doing. I sat down and leaned up against the cavern wall, sniffing myself; the odor permeating from my body smelled more like a dead skunk. *You are starting to smell worse than me.* Sarge shook his head, his tongue lolling as if he was laughing at me.

Sure. I rolled my eyes at him as he rolled over onto his back. He had been carefree ever since we started training with this group of wolves.

Harley brought over a bowl of meat and vegetables and handed it to me as he took the other to his sister. "Thanks." He nodded to me and went back to the fire to sit down. I dug into the food, feeling quite hungry after training with Hannah.

Olli came over and sat beside me, eating his food as well. We ate in silence while the others talked about the day. Fin flirted with Hannah as her brother kept giving them both an evil glance. He was protective of her, just like Sawyer was of Amora.

"Are you more confident now?" I turned my gaze to Olli, taking him in for a moment. He didn't meet my gaze, and pulling my eyes from him, I glanced down to my almost empty bowl. The steam had started to fade as the food cooled.

"Yes. I still have not caught either of the twins, though," I admitted, scooping up food with the spoon that I was using.

"I don't believe anyone would be able to catch those two." He chuckled as he placed his bowl in front of him.

I nodded. I could probably train for years with them and still not be able to keep up with or catch those two. Finishing off my food, I stood, stretching the muscles I had previously used, and exited the cave. Strolling down to the creek, I used the water to rinse out the food particles from the bowl and spoon.

Plopping down on the bank, I glanced up at the half-moon that sat in the sky. In seven days, it would be a new moon, signaling a time of renewal. I prayed to the Moon Goddess that I would soon be ready to go back to take my pack from Alpha Wade.

We will get our pack back. Don't worry about that, Nolen. Sarge was content as he laid his massive head on his front paws.

I'd like to believe that, Sarge. I really would. I continued to sit there watching the sky, wondering if Amora had even thought about me. Shaking my head to keep myself from going down the road I knew would bring me a lot of pain, a shooting star flashed by in the sky. Smiling, I closed my eyes. *I will become strong enough to take my pack back and make Amora my Luna. That I promise you.*

Standing up, I grabbed my bowl and spoon, heading back into the cave to sleep for the night. The others had started pulling out sleeping bags and settling in. Going to the back of the cave, I stripped down, allowing Sarge to take over.

I stayed warmer in his form than I did sleeping in one of those bags. Not that I got cold easily, but it was still better than being in human form. This way, I could still keep an eye out for other wolves that we didn't know.

We laid near the front of the cave entrance, curled in on ourselves. Sarge's ears swiveled, listening to the night creatures who came out at night. The sweet songs of the crickets helped us fall fast asleep.

Movement in front of us caught our attention. Opening our eyes, we kept still as we lay on the ground waiting for the sound to come again or to be able to see the person or thing making the noise.

It was still dark out as our eyes started to adjust to the dimly lit cave. We stayed still, trying to find what had woken us up. Hearing the sound again, this time out of the cave, we got up.

Stalking to the cavern entrance, we turned to glance back at the sleeping forms of the others. Deciding that it would be best to let them sleep, we continued forward. Outside the cave, we stopped, listening for more movement, before seeing a light in one of the bushes.

Staying low, we made our way to the last place the small light had been. Approaching the undergrowth, it was no longer there. Turning around, we searched with our eyes and ears.

The slivery white light flickered to my left. Sniffing the air, I made sure nothing else had been hiding in the darkness. We trotted to where the light flickered before it vanished and appeared again further down the trail. *This is getting annoying!* Irritation came through my aura as we yet again had to detour to follow the light.

Stepping out of the underbrush, we glanced around. Making sure no one else had followed us or waited for us. The light was nowhere in sight, which made me even more annoyed than following it all this way.

We were about to turn back around when the light flickered again in the middle of the field. The half-moon shone its silvery light upon the person that now stood in front of us. The silvery-haired lady softly motioned me forward. *Who is that, Sarge?*

Sarge ignored me and started to crawl up to the beautiful woman in the crystal dress. She smiled as Sarge whimpered at her.

"You took your time getting to me, Nolen."

CHAPTER EIGHTEEN: SAFE HOUSES AND ANSWERS

AMORA

I don't know how long I lay in the field that held his scent from all those months ago. But I'd been here for quite some time. Opening my eyes, I glanced around, seeing my surroundings in golds, yellows, and blues as I adjusted to my new vision.

Making myself stand, I realized I was on four legs instead of two. Glancing down at myself, the color of my legs was grey. Trotting forward to the lake that sat in the middle of the clearing, I gazed at myself; my coat was grey with a black underbelly.

Tilting my head from side to side, I stood by the lake, amazed at my wolf. *I'm glad that you love me already. We have so much time to become acquainted!*

Oh, my Goddess! This isn't a dream! You are real!

My wolf lolled her tongue, basically laughing at me. *Of course, I'm real. Why wouldn't I be, and I would never laugh at you, just with you, sweet one.*

Oh, right, I turned eighteen last night. And our mate wasn't at the party. I still don't know who he is or which pack he is from.

It's okay. We will find them. For right now, you need to eat. You haven't eaten in a while.

Okay, then let's head up to the packhouse. We made our way back up to the packhouse. I figured someone would have been trying to find me since I had been gone the whole night.

A scent caught our attention, and I couldn't place it.

Crouching low, we crawled on our belly to the edge of the forest. Sniffing around us, I realized it was the Dolostone pack. I stayed in the undergrowth as I watched them stroll right up to the packhouse.

My brother came out of the building, Danika at his side. The old Alpha of the Dolostone pack went to Sawyer. "It's time for you to step down. Otherwise, we will take your pack by force!"

"You don't have the strength to take my pack. Step foot on my territory again without asking me, and you will experience the Quartzite pack wrath." My brother stood taller, Beta Adam by his side and Delta Eric on the other.

"You young wolves think that because I'm old that I will be easily defeated. Your ally alpha of the Rhyolite pack thought he was better than me too. His death excited me, and now I have two packs, which doubles yours." The old wolf sneered at my brother, and my heart became stuck in my throat.

"Leave my pack now! When you step back on it, make sure you bring both those packs, because you will need them." I glimpsed the hurt and anger on his face as he stared down at the old wolf.

"Very well."

Staying in my hiding place until all the wolves were gone, I tried to mind link my brother. I pushed hard against his mind until he lashed out, but surprisingly, I didn't cower, though he was my alpha. I still had alpha blood as well.

"What!" He turned in my direction when I stood from my hiding place. His eyes widened in shock when he realized who I was. He ran to me; my wolf stood still as he circled her. "Mom and dad told me I couldn't come to find you. That I needed to let you grieve how you wanted. I'm sorry I wasn't there for you."

It's okay. I really needed to step away from everyone. It wasn't as bad as I thought it would be. I spoke to him through our mind link since my wolf still had control.

"Good. I need you in the packhouse now. I'm sure we will be attacked any day. Alpha Wade will be back, and he will come with what he promised. But we must be ready." We walked back to the packhouse. I was almost as tall as Sawyer in wolf form. But I knew that he would be bigger as his wolf.

Danika brought me a blanket and let me shift back to human form, the biggest smile on her face as she pulled me into a hug. I pulled away from her and smiled. "Come on, let's go inside, so Sawyer doesn't have an aneurysm."

Danika laughed, and we all made our way into the house. Excusing myself, I went up to my room so that I could get dressed. A few of the older wolves bared their necks to me, which had never happened before. *You have me now. They have to because we are alpha by blood.*

I realize that. I'm worried about the Alpha of Rhyolite pack, Nolen? I hope what that other alpha said is not true.

No reason to worry about that alpha.

I realize that, but he was a friend.

She didn't say anything else afterward as I made my way to my bedroom. Closing the door and locking it, I dropped the blanket and went to my closet. I grabbed a pair of pants and a loose T-shirt and put them on as I sighed.

Glancing around the room, I couldn't help but feel like something terrible was heading our way. My eyes landed on a photo of me, Sawyer, and Nolen. We were happy then, not a care in the world, and if anyone stared too hard at the picture, they would be able to see the slight blush on my cheeks with Nolen's arm around me.

Turning from the photo, I unlocked and exited my room. Going down the hall, I heard bits and pieces of voices on the lower landing. It sounded like my brother and Beta Adam.

"I still don't believe he is dead. He's too smart for that, and he is one of the strongest alphas I've become friends with."

"I understand that Sawyer, but anything could have happened, and Delta Eric warned him about the alpha challenge." Someone shuffled their feet, but I couldn't spot them from my position, so I decided to carefully make my way down the stairs.

"Nolen would do it again to try to protect that ungrateful pack. He would lay down his own life to protect any one of us. So, I will not believe he is dead until I see a body."

Concentrating on the conversation, I forgot about the creaky fourth step, cringing at the sound and then the glances from Sawyer and Beta Adam. I grinned at them, trying to make it not seem so awkward. "Hey, so no one has heard from Nolen yet?"

Sawyer and Beta Adam shared a glance before Beta Adam turned and left Sawyer and me in the hall. Turning to him, I placed my hands on my hips while I cocked an eyebrow at him. Sawyer took a deep breath before turning, motioning for me to follow him.

We continued down the long hall of the packhouse until we reached his office. Sawyer opened the door and stepped aside, letting me through first. I sat down on the couch, and Sawyer took a seat on the table in front of me.

"We're still trying to find Nolen. I have a few scouts roaming the areas trying to find him. I haven't given up yet, and I won't give up till I see his body." Sawyer reached for my hands as I sat on the couch, trying to figure out what to say. I mean, it had been weeks since he'd been last seen or heard from.

Glancing into Sawyer's eyes, I knew without a doubt that he would keep looking for him. "Let me go out and look too. I want to help."

Sawyer shook his head and sat back. "No, I need you here where you are safe. Because there is no telling when Alpha Wade will start his attack. I'm surprised he hasn't already, but this gives Beta Adam and Delta Eric time to get more training in."

"Do you think the Rhyolite wolves will stand with him? We are allies, after all." Sawyer stood up and started to pace before he glanced back at me.

"Nolen isn't the Alpha now. So I'm sure they would have to stand and fight against us. I believe he will make them the first line to attack."

"That's barbaric. Making a pack attack their ally."

"Unfortunately, that's how some alphas are, Amora. There are not many like Nolen."

My stomach growled, reminding me that it was still inside me and hungry. Sawyer chuckled as he went to the door; I followed him, knowing we were going to the kitchens. We start to dig through the cabinets and fridge to find something to eat. I burst out laughing as one of my memories replayed in my head. "This feels like something we would do as kids."

"Yeah! I remember when you couldn't even reach things and I had to grab them for you." Sawyer moved around the kitchen island laughing, "You were so little, and now you will find your mate one day."

"I do hope I find my mate, and I hope that he is as amazing as you said he will be." I sat there at the island, dipping Oreos in milk and snacking on chips. Sawyer scooped into the cookie dough ice cream container, sitting opposite me.

I thought his face drooped for a second before he grinned back at me. "He will, I know for a fact. Because no deadbeat would be my sister's mate."

Dolostone wolves are headed our way! The urgent mind link came through to both Sawyer and me. We left our snacks on the island, sprinting to the front doors of the house. Beta Adam and Delta Eric were standing on the steps beside Danika, the beta and delta in wolf form, as Sawyer and I approached.

Warriors to your stations! The enemy is on their way!

"Amora, go to your room!" Sawyer turned on me, his expression serious as he stared at me, willing me to do as he said.

"I will not leave my pack to sit safely in my room! I can handle myself just like anyone else!" I glared at him until he turned away from me. No one was less than me to put their life before mine if I couldn't do the same.

The gamma ran up to Sawyer, shifting from his brown wolf to his human form. "There are Dolostone wolves headed our way. There's a large number of them."

"How long do we have?"

"I'd say two days max."

"Have you found anything about the other I've asked you to look for?"

"I've picked up a trail, but it was mixed with others."

"Go back and follow that trail. And hurry, we may require more strength."

"Yes, Alpha!" He turned quickly, shifting, and ran to the east. I looked over to my brother, and he was mind linking someone.

"Danika and Amora, start going through the pack and helping the she-wolves and pups and take them to the safe house. Only let them get what they can carry. No extra."

Danika nodded and started down the steps. I wanted to be where the fighting was, not this. "Sawyer, please let me fight. I can protect you just as well as most of these males can!"

"Amora, that's why I need you with the she-wolves and pups. They are our future; please do this for me. I need you at the safe house with Danika. We haven't told many people, but she is carrying your niece or nephew. I need to be sure she is safe."

Glancing over to Danika, I could tell her scent had a subtle change to it. Turning back to Sawyer, I nodded and sprinted off to catch up with her.

Having caught back up with Danika, we made our way to the first house. She knocked on the door, and the she-wolf came to the entryway. "Bring what you can carry and head to the packhouse. We will be back after we get the other, she-wolves that are pregnant and have pups along with the older wolves."

"Yes, Luna."

We continued on to each house, telling them the same thing. When we returned to the packhouse, all the she-wolves and the pups were waiting on us. Motioning for them to follow, we helped the older wolves in first and then the heavily pregnant ones.

After the last pup was safely inside, I turned to Danika, grabbing hold of her shoulders to get her to look at me. "Go on, Danika, you as well. You need to be protected."

"I will be fine up here." She turned from me, shaking her head.

"Danika, I understand you will, but Sawyer and the pack will not. The females down in that hole need their Luna with them to protect them if they get past me." I took hold of her arms, making her look at me again. "Please go down there and help me protect you and them."

"Okay. But if you need me, I will come up."

"I need you down there." I opened the door to the safe house and made sure she made her way down, closing the door behind her and shoving the locks bolt into place. Covering the entrance with leaves and branches, I sat watching the tree line even though the enemy shouldn't be here for another day.

Nolen, where are you! We need you. I need you.

)))))🐺(((((

I shifted into my wolf later that afternoon. Sawyer had been running a mantra of orders in everyone's heads. He was starting to make my head hurt, but he was doing what any other alpha would do.

Padding through the underbrush, I kept a watch on the safe house that had been built underground to make it harder for outsiders to find us.

You know, you didn't tell me your name.

You never asked. It's Kulai. Which means Moonflower.

That's a beautiful name.

Kulai's happiness flooded through the both of us as we continued on our path. Every once in a while, I would let Sawyer know all was clear. I was about to mind link him that everything was still okay when a noise caught my attention.

The noise came again to my left, and glancing over, I saw them. Stalking through the clearing right on top of the safe house. Crouching in the bushes, someone kept pushing their mind against mine. It had to be Danika. Staying close to the ground, I opened up and pushed into Sawyer's and

Danika's minds. *Dolostone came early. They are making their way to the inner pack. They have passed the safe house. The females and pups are safe.*

Stay where you are, Amora. Keep them safe. Don't do anything stupid to get yourself killed!

After all the enemy wolves passed, I crawled out of my hiding place. Making my way to the middle of the clearing, a snarl sounded from my side, and my heart began to race. I glanced over at the wolf as it lunged at me.

Nolen

Standing there on four paws, I stared at this magical woman who knew my name as if she had known me all my life. She smiled at me before she started to stroll over to a tree stump, her dress flowing behind her, and sat down. The woman motioned for me to come to her.

Going forward as Sarge, we slowly made our way up to her. She sat on the stump, smiling at us, and once we were close to her, I felt myself shifting back to my human form. Her voice came out light and airy. "Now, that's better, isn't it?"

I looked over my body, realizing she had clothed me. Kneeling down on my knees, I bowed to this woman in the dewy grass. She had to be the Moon Goddess, the one the others were talking about. A sense of calm surrounded me when her hand touched my shoulder.

Glancing up to her beautiful face, the brightest grey eyes stared down at me. She motioned for me to stand. I stood before her, waiting for her to say something to me. She just sat there giving me curious glances, tilting her head like a wolf would.

Deciding that I would start the conversation, I took one more step closer. "I don't know what to say."

"Why don't you ask what has plagued your mind and heart for so long?" Her eyes held a bit of concern and sadness in them. She sat there on the stump, waiting on my question.

What I wanted to ask was still painful even after all these years. The sight of him lying on those steps in my mother's arms, while I could do nothing to help him. "Why did you let Archer die? Why not let me die? He would have been better for the pack. Not me."

I could feel the tears falling from my eyes. What a weak alpha I was, crying in front of the mother of all wolves. "You have never been a weak alpha, Nolen. For all you have endured, you are stronger than you believe. Archer was never to be alpha of the Rhyolite pack. They were always your pack, Nolen. Even before you were born."

I paced in front of her as I tried to make sense of what she told me. "Then why have me born second?"

"Because you had to grow up in a different manner to see things differently than the other Alphas. That is their weakness; they don't have what you have, Nolen. They are arrogant, thinking that because they are alphas, they are better than their packs. You will show them what it's like to lead a pack fairly." The Moon Goddess stood, coming up to me and placing her hands on my forearms.

"That makes no sense. I loved my brother! And you took him away from me, leaving me with a pack that hated me because I was weak in their eyes. They didn't want me as their alpha; they wanted Archer. And Sawyer is not like those other alphas; he is good and just." Glaring at her as tears now streamed down my face, I would not let her talk like that about Sawyer. He had become like a brother to me.

"I didn't take him completely away from you, my dear son. He has always been with you, and even more since you obtained your wolf. Do you think Sawyer would be the way he is now if you had not gone to his pack to train? Do you not think things would have been different if Archer was alpha and not you?" The Moon Goddess never took her eyes away from mine nor her hands from my arms. "This was both of your destinies. He would be at your side to show you how to rule a pack that did not see you for what you are."

"If you are talking about him being a part of me in my heart, then I've been told that line before. That's not the same as having him here physically." My voice cracked from all the emotion that she dredged from me. This was not what I wanted to hear. I wanted answers, not more unanswered questions.

"No, dear. He is with you because you have his wolf."

CHAPTER NINETEEN: BATTLE FOR QUARTZITE PACK

I stood there staring at her. I was so confused I couldn't make any words come out of my mouth, turning from her so I could process what she had told me. Wrapping my mind over this left me more confused than not. "His wolf was Sarge?"

"Yes."

Sarge whimpered in my head, his paws over his face. Gazing around the clearing she had brought us to, the moonflowers were blooming, emitting the most amazing scent, which I associated with Amora.

"Then the prophecy is about us. Me and Archer." The scent calmed me, bringing me back to the first kiss between Amora and me. Oh, how I wanted to have her in my arms again, pressing my lips against hers.

"Yes. You have to save the packs from the Dolostone Alpha. He has become greedy and is now wanting all wolves under him. To worship him instead of me."

I rounded on her, still more confused. "I've already fought Alpha Wade; he beat me!"

"I believe you can win this time. You have become stronger and quicker than before. All you have to do is trust in Sarge." Her hand came up to my face like my mother always did. "Our time has been quite intriguing. Go and fulfill your destiny."

I didn't know what to say to her before she disappeared. I stood there, now naked, in the clearing with the moonflowers, their scent all around me. I had to get to the cave and let them know we needed to leave now.

Taking one last deep breath of the moonflowers scent, I shifted and raced through the woods to the cave. Pushing myself and Sarge through the underbrush as fast as I could.

Why didn't you tell me?

I tried. Your brother said you were smart. So I figured dropping hints would help.

Really? Hints!

What? It's not like I could tell you straight out. Selene told me I couldn't say anything to you. Not until she was able to talk to you. I'm sorry.

Don't be. You were only following orders.

The pounding of our feet on the forest floor rang in our ears. The sun rose over the trees, its bright pinks and oranges painting the sky just as I made it to the entrance of the cave. The others were up, and another male was with them.

I recognized this platinum blond wolf! He was Sawyer's gamma! Shifting quicker than I had ever done, I entered the cave. Olli glanced up first and then Fin with his signature stoic face.

Sawyer's gamma turned to find out what they were staring at, and when he saw me, he jumped up and ran to me. "I'm so glad I found you! We need to go now. The Dolostone Alpha wants to fight our pack. We need you and anyone else willing to fight."

Glancing over to the others, Ollie's eyes connected with mine, and he nodded. My gaze swept over each of the wolves that had helped me during this time as they stood up, nodding to me. "Okay, let's go. How far are we from the pack?"

"A day if we don't stop. Hopefully, the Dolostone pack hasn't started the attack yet."

"When did he say he would attack?"

"It took me a day to get here. Which was the day he threatened to attack. If we leave now, we could sneak in under darkness where the safe house is."

"Then we need to hurry because I guarantee that he attacked early."

The gamma nodded, then shifted, and I shifted after him. The others followed us, and we took off out of the cave after the Gamma to get to the Quartzite pack.

We arrived at the back of the Quartzite lands around dark. The fighting sounded as if it was coming from the front part of the pack. That's when I spotted the wolf body on the ground in the center of the clearing.

With her scent everywhere, I panicked and rushed forward as the others called out to me to stop. As I got to the body, its scent started to mix with Amora's. This was not her, but she had been here, and her scent had intensified since she had turned eighteen.

MATE!

Her aroma calmed me and excited me all at once. Seeing the dead body of the male wolf and its throat ripped out gave me some comfort that she was still alive. Glancing over my shoulder, I motioned with my head for them to follow me.

We stalked through the back of the territory and rounded the pack-house. The commotion from the battle rang in our ears. Snarls and yelps came from the territory's east, which spurred us on faster. Bodies littered the ground as we sprinted to the battle now in progress.

Joining the fray, I began tearing into wolves I didn't recognize. Ripping throats and limbs from massive bodies. I glimpsed Sawyer fighting with two brown wolves. Darting over, I lunged at the wolf in the air, knocking him into a tree with a crunch.

Landing on my feet, I turned just as Sawyer finished off the other wolf, and he swung around on me, snarling. I snorted, bringing him out of the fight or flight mentality he was in. That's when he finally noticed it was me. Giving me a nod, we both went back into the fray of battle.

We worked together, fighting the Dolostone wolves off the other wolves. I spotted some of the Rhyolite wolves mixed with them; once they saw me, they stopped battling the Quartzite wolves and rounded on the Dolostone wolves. Tearing and slashing with renewed vigor; they were a little skinny, but they fought hard.

Some of my pack had lost their lives and were bleeding out on the ground. My heart constricted at the sight, but there was nothing I could do now other than fight to take them back from Alpha Wade. Sarge whimpered before getting his head back into the fight.

We will make him pay for what he has done!

You got that right, buddy!

Wolves attacked Sawyer and me from all sides, trying their best to take both of us down. Sawyer fought alongside me just like we did when we'd trained together. Beta Adam took down a wolf at his side, ripping its throat out. He glanced up at Sawyer, and I was sure his jaw would have dropped if he were in human form. Beta Adam gave me a quick nod before he tore into another wolf.

Surveying the battle around me for a second, I spotted Alpha Wade fighting with a mixture of Quartzite and Rhyolite wolves. Nipping Sawyer, I motioned with my head to the other alpha. He nodded, and we rushed in to help the warrior wolves. As we got closer to him, he saw me running with Sawyer, grabbed one of the Rhyolite wolves, and flung him at us.

We jumped in unison over the warrior wolf as the others scattered while he took off and ran in the other direction. *Coward!* Sarge snarled as he quickened his pace. Dolostone wolves cut off our advance, and I glanced over to Sawyer, who growled at the wolves. Some of them whimpered but held their ground as others snarled back at us.

Sarge, he's getting away! Sarge continued to snarl and snap his jaws as we watched Alpha Wade run from the battle. Some of the Dolostone wolves followed him. Sawyer and I inched back until both the Rhyolite and Quartzite packs surrounded them. The wolves in the circle shifted back to their human forms, their hands covering the back of their heads as they lay on the ground in surrender.

Sawyer raised his head, letting out a long howl. Others joined him throughout the territory. The sound of victory rang through the land as wolves shifted back to humans. I shifted back as well; blood covered me from head to toe, Sawyer similarly drenched.

My friend moved toward me, a smile plastered on his face. He grabbed me into a bear hug; if he hadn't been like a brother to me, I would have thought this was a little weird. Pulling away from me, he held me at arm's length. "I knew you were alive. There was no way you could've been dead. I never gave up searching for you!"

"I felt that way for a few weeks. Until I met up with some rogues that taught me more than what I knew." Smiling back at him, I glanced over his shoulder at the group of wolves I had been with since I lost my way. "I want you to meet them. Come on."

We made our way over to them, and they all bowed their head. "Sawyer, this is Olli, Fin, Markus, Hannah, and Harley. Guys, this is Sawyer, the Alpha of Quartzite pack and my best friend."

Rhyolite wolves came up and surrounded us, all of them on one knee. It seemed like most of the pack that had been in the battle made it. Even in human form, they were skin and bones.

He starved my pack and then made them attack their ally! I will destroy him and bring my pack back to their former selves. Kneeling down in front of the red-headed male before me, I raised his sunken face. "Lucas! Where's Daylen and Axel?"

"Daylen is here somewhere." His voice was raspy from non-use. His eyes were cloudy, when they had used to be so full of life.

"Axel?" Lucas's shoulders began to shake as he stared back at me, tears welling up in his eyes.

"He's dead. Wade killed him after he refused to be his beta. Left him on the ground for scavengers to pick at him while he rotted in front of the packhouse as a warning to anyone who went against him. I want to avenge his death."

"We will. We will avenge all our brothers and sisters that he has taken from us. I promise you that." I grasped his hand pulled him to stand. Glancing over my starved pack, I couldn't help but feel like I had failed them even more with them in the state there were in. "If you will take me back, Rhyolite pack, I promise you will never know hunger again; I will go hungry before you will."

The Rhyolite wolves looked at Lucas, and he gazed back at me. "There's no better leader than you, Nolen. It might have been short, but we all appreciated that you tried to save us from battle with the Alpha challenge. Each and every one of us wants you back."

Nodding, I clapped him on the shoulder, fighting back the emotions that threatened to make themselves known. I spotted Daylen running up, and relief filled me knowing that my Delta and Gamma were still alive. "What about my parents? Are they still alive?"

Daylen spoke up, winded from his run to me. "Yes, they were still alive when we left. I don't know if they will spare them if we attack them."

Sighing, I rubbed the back of my neck, trying to figure out what I should do. My pack was starving, and I realized they wouldn't be able to make it in another battle so soon. "Nolen, I have your back, man. We will take back the Rhyolite pack together like we always do. We are allies, and you're practically my brother. I would do anything for you and your pack."

"Thank you, Sawyer. That means a lot to me."

"No question, brother! You mean a lot to us, and we will always be your allies."

The scent of moonflowers invaded my senses, and I began to search for her, knowing she was somewhere close. That's when I spotted her helping another wolf out of the woods; blood covered her perfect body and matted her hair. Her head snapped up, and her beautiful amber eyes locked with mine.

"Mate!"

CHAPTER TWENTY: FIRSTS

Amora

After the battle ended, Kulai became frantic, pacing in my head. As I was helping an injured wolf out of the woods, I noticed the most intoxicating scent ever to reach my nose. I looked up, and my eyes locked with his familiar deep blue ones. My heart raced as I stood staring at the person I had wanted the most since I was a young girl.

"Mate!" Kulai was ecstatic in my head. I couldn't believe he was here after all this time! He was a little leaner than the last time I saw him, but, damn, he was still just as gorgeous!

Helping the injured wolf down to the ground near the other injured wolves, I finally ran to him. I didn't see anyone but him and his handsome smile. Colliding into him, his arms wrapped around me, pulling me closer than I'd ever been against him.

Breaking the embrace, I glanced up at him. I couldn't believe this male, this alpha, was mine! The male I had been dreaming of was mine!

"Mate." My voice came out as a whisper, but Nolen grinned anyway. His hand came up to my face and gently caressed my cheek. He was being so gentle with me when all I wanted him to do was take me to my room, mate me, and possibly mark me. Placing one hand on his and the other on his chest, he shivered. The electricity between us intensified. "Nolen, it's you, and you're mine."

"Yes. Always have been." His voice was a deep baritone, and his eyes flickered between his deep blues and his wolf's soft golden color.

"Why didn't you tell me? You knew, and you didn't tell me." It hurt that he'd kept it a secret from me. Did he not want me? Did he not think I was worthy?

"I wanted to, but I had to keep it from you until you sensed it as well. There is a law about younger mates that forbade me from telling you. I told my parents about you, and I assumed they told your parents." His other hand went to the other side of my face. I wanted Nolen so bad, and I could tell he wanted me too. The pupils of his eyes had widened, and they changed to his wolf's every few seconds.

"Then make up for it! Take me! I don't care where, just take me!" I grabbed hold of the back of his hair, pulling his body back against mine. His eyes cut to the right side of him, then back to me. Nolen's heart raced underneath his ribcage bounding against my chest.

"I want to, but I don't want you to be in pain if I die. I won't do that to you." Nolen tried to kiss me, but I pulled away and shook my head. He wasn't going to get off that easy.

"No, you will not go off to fight Wade without taking me first. I won't let you go if you don't." Kulai agreed with me as she lay there on her side in my head, her tail beating against the ground. I stared at him in his eyes, the ones I always became lost in.

"Amora." His eyes held a mixture of emotion in them. I knew he was trying to make an excuse to not take me when I knew he wanted me just as bad as I wanted him.

"No, you won't leave. I won't let you! You will not leave till you make me all yours!" I realized I was being a child in the way that I spoke to him. But I couldn't let him go when I just got him back.

Nolen glanced over to his right again, and I realized he was looking to Sawyer on what to do. I saw Sawyer shrug out of my peripheral before Nolen brought his gaze back to mine. "Okay, but I have to take care of my pack that is here first. Then I'm all yours."

Nodding, I took a step back until he pulled me back into him and pressed a punishing kiss to my lips, which made me light-headed when he pulled away and grabbed ahold of my earlobe. "Go get cleaned up, and I'll be up shortly. If you stand here one more second, I might get jealous that other males are seeing what's mine."

Blushing at the thought of both him taking me and realizing I was still naked, I took off to the packhouse. Sawyer's laughter rang out behind me. Taking a chance, I glanced back at Nolen, whose lust-filled gaze stared back at me, making sure I went into the packhouse.

My heart raced as I jumped in the shower. I was nervous about what was to come, but I was so ready! Nolen was mine. The Goddess must have heard my insistent pleas. The door to my room opened and his scent carried through the air to me.

His soft footsteps became more evident the closer he got to the bathroom. I opened the shower door to peek out and saw him standing in the doorway. He was still covered in blood. "Are you going to come in or are you just going to stand there?"

My gaze roamed his body, taking in every movement of his muscles as he strolled toward me. Before today, I had never exactly stared at a naked man before, but none would compare to him. As he stepped inside the shower, his proximity gave me goosebumps. The water fell against his hard body, rinsing some of the blood and dirt from his skin. "Nolen, let me wash you?"

Nolen nodded, his eyes never leaving mine as I grabbed my loofah and pumped the soap from the bottle on it. I began to rub him down, lathering his skin with the soap. His moans brought my eyes back to his face, he leaned his head back, and his eyes were half-mast. "Does this feel good?"

Nolen's eyes flew open at the sound of my voice, and I thought I heard a rumble come from him. He stepped back into the cascading water, the bubbles running down his now clean body. He placed both his hands on the sides of my face. "You are so beautiful!"

"Are you nervous?" We hadn't gotten out of the shower, and I didn't know what he was thinking. Nolen grinned and then shook his head.

"I've never been nervous around you. Just worried you didn't want me the way I wanted you." He traced his thumb over my lips, which made me immediately wet them with my tongue. His touch was soft against my skin, like he was afraid to break me.

"I feel stupid for saying this, but I've been drawn to you ever since you came to Quartzite. I didn't understand how I could be so attached to someone when I wasn't of age." I dropped my gaze from him to watch my fingers trace his wolf yin and yang tattoo.

Nolen grabbed my loofah, pumping some of my body wash on it, and began scrubbing the blood from my body. We switched places and rinsed the dried blood from my hair with the warm water. He continued to wash me, and when he went down to wash my center, he no longer used the loofah. Nolen's hands were like silk against my folds, rubbing and massaging me, leaving me struggling to stay standing. I rested my hands on his shoulders when one of his fingers dipped inside.

Turning around to face the water, I brought his hand back down to help me rinse the soap out. Nolen's fingers felt so much better than my own as he rubbed me. Arching into him, a moan escaped me as I wrapped my arms around his neck, and he held me against him. His mouth found my neck, and he nipped and sucked on it while his hand played down below, working me into a frenzy.

"Nolen, I think I'm cumming!"

Nolen chuckled and nipped me harder, removing his hand from my pussy. "Uh-uh, not right now."

The shower turned off, and Nolen stepped over to grab a towel. He brought it over to me, and started to dry me off, his lips touched my neck, and he made his way down to the spot where my mark would be placed. The further he went with the towel, his lips followed.

He took the towel and dried himself, throwing it over the rod. Nolen then grabbed me up, and I wrapped my legs around his waist. I could feel his cock against me, and I couldn't help but be excited. He exited the bathroom with me placing soft kisses along my neck and upper chest.

The moan slipped out before I could stop it, and my face became slightly red. When Nolen glanced up at me, his pupils had completely taken over his blues. He took me over to my bed and laid me in the middle. There was no way anyone couldn't smell the arousal in this room because it was pooling down below, readying me for what it wanted most. Nolen climbed up on the bed with me, settling himself between my legs before he kissed me.

My hands wrapped around his neck as the desire from his kiss became more passionate. He broke the kiss and peppered my skin with small open-mouthed pecks, making his way down to the inside of my thighs before he glanced up at me. "You okay with this?"

I nodded because I knew I would not be able to utter a word, and when he seized my clit with his mouth, I had never experienced such pleasure. My hands went to his head as he sucked on the little nub that brought me so much gratification, causing my legs to spasm. Nolen widened my legs and rested them on his shoulders as his hands went to my ass, lifting my lower half closer to his face.

When his tongue parted the folds and entered inside me, I thought I was going to explode! Holy shit! "Nolen!" He stopped to glance up at me, and I groaned due to his lack of touch. His face was full of concern as he stared back at me, slowly lifting his mouth away from my clit.

"What's wrong?"

"Nothing, it was perfect."

He grinned at me as he lowered my ass down and moved back up, leaning on his arms. He captured my lips with his while he pushed his tongue inside my mouth, and I pressed back against him. I ran my hands along his back when I felt him at my entrance. I couldn't say if it was bigger than average or smaller since I hadn't been with anyone before now. "Are you ready? I don't want to hurt you."

"I've been ready." Bringing a hand up to his face, I ran my fingers along the hard edges of his face. Nolen sat upon his knees, lining himself up; he glanced back up to me, and I gave him a nod. He grabbed hold of my hips as he entered me. My hands went to his wrists as I tried to breathe through the uncomfortable feeling of having him inside me. He stopped for a moment, letting his gaze roam my naked body below him. I knew he didn't want to hurt me, so I decided to help him break it myself. Wrapping my legs around his waist, I plunged him deeper into me.

It didn't hurt nearly as bad as I had been told. The groan that came from Nolen when I sheathed him made me smile to myself. His hands on my hips tightened, and his eyes were closed. I raised my hand to his face, caressing his cheek. He opened his eyes, and I realized they were the golden color of his wolf's.

Wrapping my fingers behind his head, I pulled him down on top of me. Nolen enveloped me in his arms, bringing us closer to each other. He started to kiss me again before he began moving inside me, and, Goddess, did it make me quake! I moved with him, getting in rhythm with his thrusts quickly.

Nolen's movements became faster, along with my own, more insistent with the coming pleasure that tore down inside me. My pussy contracted around him, decreasing the circumference he had to move inside of me. My body tensed as the sense of fulfillment rushed out just as Nolen's own satisfaction spilled into me. Without hesitation, my canines ripped from my gums, and I plunged them into Nolen's mating spot. He followed after, and the gratification of it made me cum again.

Pulling out, I licked the small amount of blood from his shoulder and sealed my mark. No female would be able to take this male from me. Nolen closed his mark on me and rolled off me while pulling me to his side.

Snuggling into his side, I glanced up at him while I ran my hand over his chest. Humming to myself, Nolen's chest rumbled underneath my hand. "Why are you staring at me."

"I was just wondering if I was your first." Staring at him in his gorgeous blue eyes, he smiled back at me. He grabbed my hand, kissed it, and placed a kiss on the top of my head.

"You are my first and last."

I sighed contently as I fell fast asleep in his arms.

His breath fanned my ear as his whispered baritone professed, "I love you, Amora."

Nolen

Laying there in her bed with her in my arms was a dream come true. I had waited so long for her to turn of age so she could sense the bond as I did. Yet we'd both felt some form of it before we turned eighteen. Amora had fallen asleep, and my body was on its way to blacking out as well. I was exhausted, between the run back here, the battle, and sex with Amora. Sarge was content in my head, sleeping away while I lay there thinking back on the last twenty-four hours.

So much had changed for me, and I didn't know what the next forty-eight hours would show us. Selene had told me it was my destiny to fight Wade to protect the packs from his unjust rule. But would I be ready? The part of my pack that had come to fight was now having probably their first authentic meal in days.

Sawyer and I had decided to give them and his pack two days to rest up and get prepared to fight. The only thing was—Alpha Wade had the same amount of time to do the same. My parents were still there, and I didn't know if he would slaughter them to get back at me. The thought of my mother in those dungeons pissed me off! I would kill Wade if he had hurt one hair on her head.

Amora snuggled further into me, mixing her scent into the air. My heart swelled at the sight of her, pushing the hair out of her beautiful face. *Goddess, you couldn't have picked a more wonderful mate than her.*

I pulled up the quilt to cover us to keep anyone who walked in the room from seeing our naked bodies. Well, mainly hers, I thought with a smile. Closing my eyes, I finally let myself fall asleep.

CHAPTER TWENTY-ONE: TRAITOR

AMORA

Strong arms enveloped me as a sense of peace surrounded me, and when I opened my eyes, they fell upon his handsome serene face. The sharp lines of his jaw were more prominent since he had been rogue, but it was clear Nolen was at peace after weeks on the run. I reached up softly, tracing his face before kissing him on the lips.

Nolen's arms tightened around me as he met my kiss with more passion. The kiss alone made my body heat up, encouraging me to take him again for round two. He broke our kiss, and our eyes met, flickering between his and his wolf's color. I grinned, bringing my lips up to his again for a peck. "Good morning, mate."

"Good morning." Nolen chuckled at my raspy voice as he pushed back some of my hair from my face. I couldn't get over the look he gave me every time he stared at me. How could I have missed these looks? His smile and that passion in his eyes were there every moment we had shared in the past, and I was too naïve to realize he was giving me hints. "So, what do you have planned today with my brother?"

"I plan to be right here with you until the last possible moment." Nolen pulled me over on top of him. We were both still naked, and his cock throbbed underneath me. His hands ran over my skin, followed by his eyes, I blushed when they reached my pussy, and they lingered there longer than the other places. Nolen's fingers caressed the little nub, and I shuddered with need when he inserted two fingers inside me. He stroked my G-spot until I was close to orgasm, then pulled them out at the last moment.

Someone pressed their mind against mine, and I tried to ignore them, but they were insistent. Bringing my attention back to Nolen, I halted his hands and lips. "Someone is trying to mind link me. I need to answer them."

Nolen sighed as he rested his hands on my hips. I opened my mind to the person interrupting the pleasure my mate was giving me. *About time you answer. We need you and Nolen down here in the office.*

Really! The sun isn't even up, and we were busy!

Amora, I want both your asses down here now. There is a problem with Nolen's pack.

Fine.

I cut the link and returned my gaze back to Nolen. He cocked his head to the side with a mischievous grin. As much as I wanted to continue what we had been doing, we needed to head down to find out what was going on. "Sawyer needs us in his office. Something about your pack."

Nolen sighed and sat up, and with one swift motion, he stood with me in his arms. I giggled as he placed kisses along my neck, and when he got to my mark, my core tightened as the pleasure from his mouth coerced a moan from my lips. Grabbing his face, I brought it up to mine as Nolan continued into the closet. He sat me on my feet and caressed my cheek with a chuckle. "I know, Amora. Let's get dressed and see what my pack has gotten themselves into now."

We walked hand and hand to my brother's office. Each wolf we passed bowed their heads. Glancing at Nolen from the corner of my eye, I realized that he was focused in front of him as we made our way down the stairs to the bottom floor. The sparks that still ignited from our touch made me want to turn us around and head back to my bedroom, but I pushed that ever-consuming feeling down.

I had never realized that the hall was so long before, though it could be that I just wanted him to myself. Nolen's grip tightened on my hand, bringing my attention back to him. Gazing up at him, he was smiling at me; we had reached my brother's office door, and I could tell that something wasn't right.

Entering the office, my brother was sitting at the desk while two warriors had hold of Nolen's delta between them, his head held low. Nolen's demeanor changed as his gaze flitted between his Delta and my brother. Danika was behind Sawyer, along with Beta Adam and Nolen's gamma. Lucas was standing on the other side of the room. His face red with anger, his eyes blazing with his wolf's, his gaze turned to Nolen, and when their eyes met, he bared his neck and kept his eyes down. "What's going on, Sawyer?"

"My guards found Daylen in the cells trying to release the surrendered wolves of Dolostone. He also admitted to something I believe he should tell you himself." Sawyer stood from his desk and made his way to us. He glanced at me, and I nodded, letting go of Nolen's hand and standing on tiptoe. I kissed him, and he kissed me back. I turned from my brother and my mate and went over to Danika.

Nolen went up to the Delta and forced him to lift his head. The expression on his face told me that Nolen's wolf was at the surface, and at this moment, death could be soon for the Rhyolite wolf. "Why were you trying to free the very people that enslaved your pack members?"

"They are not my pack anymore. I switched sides. They promised me that if I helped Alpha Wade take you down, I would have the Beta position of that territory. You and your dad were not doing anything with the threat he made. I gave you wolfsbane days before Alpha Wade came to make you surrender the pack. But like always, it wasn't enough. So, when you were fighting him, I injected it into your thigh while you were distracted." I couldn't believe what this wolf was telling Nolen and how he kept eye contact with him. He apparently had a death wish. I grasped Danika's hand, and she tightened her grip on mine. Luckily Nolen had Sawyer behind him, but I was not too sure if that was a good thing or a bad thing at the moment.

Nolen's anger washed over me, and I realized he was going to attack before he did it, and I felt sorry for the wolves holding the Delta. He had the male from his pack against the wall, his face turning blue from the lack of oxygen. "You did what!! You low-life mother fucker!! What about my parents? You were supposedly taking care of them!"

Sawyer just stood there watching as his best friend held one of his packmates against the wall. I couldn't take it any longer and pushed past Sawyer and laid my hands on Nolen's flesh, bringing his attention back to me. His face was contorted in anger, and his eyes flashed his wolf's before softening. "Nolen, this is not you. You are better than this. This is what he wants from you, don't you understand that?"

Nolen kept my gaze as his face changed back to his gorgeous features. His eyes were the last turn, back to his beautiful blue eyes. Nolen turned back to the Delta and dropped him in a heap against the wall, holding his already bruising neck. "Take him away and throw him in the cells with his new pack. He is no longer a Rhyolite wolf."

The two warriors nodded and grabbed him back up, dragging him toward the prison. Once they were away from us, I moved over to stand in front of him. His eyes had a faraway glaze to them, and I realized that he was worried about his parents. Reaching up, I brushed my fingertips over his cheek, and he leaned against my hand as he brought his up and over mine. "We will find out what happened to your parents, and we will take out any wolf that had anything to do with your downfall."

Nolen smiled before placing a chaste kiss on my lips and turning to Sawyer. He kept me tight against his side; my brother's eyes glanced at my mark and then Nolen's before his boyish grin grew on his lips. "What do you think our plan of action needs to be now? I'm all for going to war now and showing that asshole what we are made of."

"Yeah, but what happens if we don't have the strength or the rest of the pack that stayed behind wants to be in his pack? I want to rescue my parents, but I'm afraid they have already been killed." Nolen and Sawyer stared at each other as I stood there at his side. This was where I was meant to be, by his side for the rest of my life. It was what I dreamed of—being with him, and that dream had come true. Prayers really did come true!

"We will call a pack meeting. Gather everyone and see what they think. We leave right after the meeting if they are all for it." Sawyer turned to Beta Adam and Nolen's gamma. They both nodded, and their eyes glazed over as they both spoke to their respective packs. When their eyes readjusted, they nodded again. Sawyer reached out his hand, and Danika placed her hand in his. She was glowing, which made me want to have a pup soon as well.

Nolen nudged me, and I glanced up at him; his brows were furrowed with his head tilted to the side. A laugh escaped my lips at his expression, which only made him that much more confused. Shaking my head, I pulled him forward to walk behind Sawyer and Danika. "What's wrong?"

"Nothing." Thinking about having a pup this soon should not be on my mind as we were faced with a war between packs. I smiled up at him as he gazed down at me. There were a few times I had to keep him from running into someone. As we all filed into the big hall, the pack members made their way into the packhouse. This meeting would be a hard one.

Nolen and Sawyer stood closer to the edge of the stage, while Danika and I sat in a couple of chairs to the side and Beta Adam and Lucas, Nolen's gamma, stood on the other side of the two Alphas. Sawyer called for order once everyone was in the hall, silencing the murmuring.

"Quartzite and Rhyolite pack, we have called this meeting as we have received disastrous news." The murmuring picked up again as Sawyer gazed over our pack and Nolen's. He held up his hands again, quieting the wolves before us. "This morning, we found the Delta of the Rhyolite pack trying to free the captured Dolostone wolves. He admitted to being a spy for them, and we need to decide whether we attack now, today, or wait until tomorrow. We know you all are tired. We are too. But if you want our lives back the way they were, we need to take action and fast. What do you say?" The wolves before us stood there in silence. Some spoke quietly to their neighbor. We all waited for the answer. Many were unsure, I could see it on their faces. A younger wolf from Nolen's pack stepped forward, determination set on his face.

"Alpha Nolen, Alpha Sawyer, I will stand with you to fight to take my home back the way it was when Alpha Nolen was still in power. I'm not going to let my sisters and brothers starve because I'm too afraid to stand up to a tyrant. I vote we go today! The sooner we defeat Alpha Wade, the sooner I can see my siblings again." Wolves from both packs seemed to be taken aback by the bold young wolf, but a few others from the Rhyolite pack waded through the crowd and came forward, kneeling and bearing their necks. Quartzite wolves stepped forward as well, and my heart swelled with pride at them.

Nolen stepped forward, a smile on his face. I could sense the pride he held for this rag-tag part of his pack, and it seeped through to the others. "Thank you, Zac. Rhyolite, Quartzite, we leave now. Grab what you need for battle and be prepared to leave within the hour. I appreciate each and every one of you. No matter what pack you are in, we are all family!"

The pack of wolves cheered after his comment, and the wolves going with us began to hug loved ones and go to their houses to obtain what they needed. I stood, going up to Nolen. Linking my hand in his made him glance down with a smile. "We should head up and grab our stuff."

"I want you to stay here, Amora. To help protect the pack here and protect Danika." Furious, I jerked my hand from his and took a step back. I knew he was not trying to sideline me.

"No. I refuse to stay here. The Rhyolite pack will be my pack as well when WE defeat Wade. I will not stay here with my tail between my legs while others fight! I'm an alpha too, and I will go." Stomping my foot on the stage shook the floor under us; a few of the wolves that stayed in the big hall turned their attention to me. Nolen glanced over to Sawyer, and I saw him shrug from my peripherals.

Nolen sighed and then ran his hand over his face. He glanced back at me, and I could see a slight smirk begin on his lips. "As much as my wolf demands me to lock you in your room. You are right. You will be their

Luna, and you are also an alpha by blood. But if you come, you have to stay close to Lucas. I don't know what I'd do if I lost you!"

CHAPTER TWENTY-TWO: TAKING BACK RHYOLITE PACK

The packs were assembled in the front of the packhouse as Sawyer and I stood in front of them, dividing them into regiments. We left one to defend the pregnant she-wolves, pups, and older wolves, who had gone back into the underground safe house. Danika was not too thrilled that she was back in there. But with her carrying the heir of the Quartzite pack, she had no choice. Once we had everyone where they needed to be, we shifted and made our way to Alpha Wade and my territory.

Amora's wolf ran beside us, and Lucas ran at her left flank. Sawyer was on my other side; I would have enjoyed this if we weren't running to our possible deaths. Her wolf was as beautiful as she was, and the way her coloring spread it made me believe we were really made for each other in every sense of the word.

Where Sarge was black, she was grey and the same with my grey and her black. Her eyes were amber, just like in her human form, and she was bigger than most she-wolves. But she was still not as large as Sawyer or me.

Getting closer to the pack border, our unit's right and left sides split off, skirting the edge to flank the Dolostone wolves, while Sawyer and I took Amora, Lucas, and my new friends onward. Glancing over my shoulder, I nodded to Hannah and Harley. They both had a particular job to do since they were the fastest, and I hoped we weren't too late.

They both broke off and ran ahead, weaving through the trees and underbrush until I could no longer see them. Fin, Olli, and Markus continued with us as we slowed and made our way stealthily over the pack border. It had started to turn dark, and everything was quiet as we tramped on further into the pack land.

Blood and decaying flesh floated to us just as we made it to the wood line. Sarge snarled softly, making Amora's wolf come up to him and nuzzle him. *We will make Wade pay for what he has done to our pack!*

No sound reached us; the territory was eerily silent. Which made me worry about the pack members here. Glancing over to Lucas, I tilted my head; we couldn't actually communicate in wolf form until I took the pack back from Wade and became alpha again.

Lucas's eyes glazed over for a few seconds before he gazed back over to me. He shifted back to his human form and kneeled beside me, his hand on my massive shoulder. "The pack is there but are unsure if Dolostone is still here since they told the others to get in their homes and not come back out."

Sawyer shifted, and then I did. I glanced over at Lucas and then at Sawyer. I didn't like that the land was so quiet, I turned to Amora's wolf, crouched low in the bushes. "Sawyer, ask the wolves that went to the rear if they have seen anything. I don't see Wade running back here and not trying to fight to keep the territory."

Sawyer's eyes glazed over as he conversed with someone from his pack. We all waited, watching for anything that might force us to shift. Sawyer turned to me, his eyes back to their usual color. "They haven't seen anything on their end either. We need to take a few wolves with us and scout the inner part of the pack territory."

I nodded, turning to search for Olli, Fin, and Markus. Finding them, I motioned for them to come to me. I glanced around at them, trying to figure out what needed to be done. "Alright, you guys. I need you all to come with Sawyer and me. Lucas stays here with Amora, and I'll signal when everyone needs to attack."

Lucas nodded, and I was pretty sure Amora rolled her eyes at me, but she kept quiet. Turning to Sawyer, I gave him a brief nod before shifting back to Sarge. Sawyer and Lucas shifted back as well. Lucas went to Amora and stood beside her, while Sawyer and I, along with the other three wolves, snuck out of the wood line and into the clearing where the training fields were.

This field was once beautiful and lively as pups trained on it. Now it held decaying bodies and bones from my pack. The stench alone masked our scent as we stalked further inward. Each rustle of sound stalled our progress through the territory. The town's stores were closed, but I noticed a curtain move back into place at the top of one of the store's apartments.

We were almost to the packhouse when I caught mother's scent in the air. It was faint and masked with the smell of urine and feces, but I could tell it was her. When we rounded the corner, I spotted Alpha Wade standing at the top of the steps, my mother on her knees as a warrior wolf held her by her knotted and matted hair at his side.

Tears streamed down her face as she spotted the group of wolves at my side and me. A cruel sneer held its place on Alpha Wade's face. I wanted to claw this wolf to pieces for what he had done to my mother! Her face was cut and bruised as if someone had been hitting her, and I would find out who.

I nudged Sawyer, and he slunk back, and Fin took his place. His lips were drawn up away from his teeth, but no sound came from the white wolf. Wade kept his gaze on me. I was hoping that Sawyer would be able to reach the wolves that were at the edge of the territory without alerting Wade that he was mind linking them. "So, you thought you would sneak up on me? Too bad one of your little omegas saw you in town and is mated to one of my warriors."

So, some of my people have mates in the Dolostone pack. That could prove problematic for me. Especially if the Dolostone wolf was extremely loyal to their alpha, I didn't know what I would do but keeping them apart was not something I would consider. Staring back at the old wolf, I tried to keep my gaze from going to my mother. That wolf would pay for hurting my mother. I felt the nip to my tail and began to shift back to my human form. "I can't help what a mate does for their other half. But if you think that I will just sit back and let you take packs, you are wrong."

The old Alpha laughed and went over to the warrior holding my mother, a sinister smirk on his lips. He grabbed hold of my mother's arm and forced her to stand. The other wolf stepped back away from his alpha. "Tell me, Nolen, what do you think will happen to your mother if you try to take back these weak wolves? As we speak, your dad is hanging by his wrists in silver chains."

My mother whimpered, which made me even angrier. A cold, wet nose pressed into my palm, I glanced over, and Sawyer's eyes met mine. Nodding to him, I brought my gaze back to my mother. "Wade, you're going to wish that you had never come across our packs. Because today you will cease to exist."

Letting Sarge back in control, we shifted in seconds and quickly ran to my mother. I spotted Hannah speeding toward us on my right side. Alpha Wade had his full attention on me and didn't realize Hannah was on him until she ran between him and my mother. My mother was knocked free and grabbed hold of Hannah's fur, and she took off to the woods.

My jump landed me on top of Wade, and I grabbed him by the arm between my teeth, throwing him as wolves poured out of the woods and packhouse. Massive bodies clashed against each other as Wade shifted in mid-air, staggering as he landed on four paws.

I rushed him as he came toward me, brandishing his fangs as saliva ran down the white ivory bone. He had years on me, but I was stronger in my youth. Using my massive paw, I swiped at his face, knocking him to the side and off the porch. He got up quicker than I thought he would, but I met him in the middle of the stairs, grabbing hold of one of his ears and slinging him to the side once more.

The snarls and growls and yelps from the wolves around us were background noise to me. All that was on my mind was Wade and how I would dispatch him from this world for taking my brother, my pack, and my title from me. This wolf would have no mercy from me; he would only understand the pain and the person who gave it.

Wade got up slowly this time but rushed me again, grabbing hold of a clump of fur from my neck and ripping it out. Sarge snarled, snapping his teeth at the wolf before him. This time, we charged him, grabbing hold of his leg and snapping it between our massive jaws. His yelp came quick, and he staggered backward; he would have no help this time to take me down. I would show him what real power was like as I took his life from him.

This will be for Archer. I will avenge his death with the death of this man, I pledged to Sarge. He surged forward, his massive muscles strained under skin and fur, sending him quicker to the brown wolf that stood on three legs waiting for us. I was almost upon him when I heard her yelp, bringing my attention to the grey and black wolf and grey wolf that fought near the side of the garden by the packhouse.

Lucas had a hold of the brown wolf whose teeth were around my mate's paw. Lucas kept inching his teeth closer and closer to the attacking wolf's throat. I ran to them without hesitation, sinking my teeth into the other side of the wolf's neck, yanking out a pound of flesh. After the wolf dropped to the ground, I went up to my mate. Licking her paw and nestling into her neck.

Lucas stood guard over us as I made sure that Amora was fine. I licked her paw once more before searching for the other alpha. His wolves had started to surrender, shifting back to their human form, kneeling on the ground. Spotting the Dolostone Alpha running away again, I sprinted after him. He was not going to get away this time.

I sprinted through the underbrush, him stumbling as Sarge leaped and weaved through it. Gaining on him, we lunged, grabbing hold of the back of his neck with my teeth and, using my weight, pulled him down into the dirt. We fought on the ground. Sarge tore into him as he tried to stand. He finally used his feet to push me off him.

His blood dripped from my mouth as it poured from his wounds. Hair was scattered in the dirt and bushes as we snarled at each other. Howls sounded out in victory from the Quartzite and Rhyolite packs. Wade's eyes searched the trees while his ears swiveled, listening for anything other than the howling.

I took that moment and charged, coming under his head, and latching my teeth around his jugular. Shaking and tearing at his throat, his blood poured down on my face like a waterfall. The older Alpha fell to the ground; his eyes glanced up at me before the life faded from them.

I raised my head to the sky and howled at the moon. Letting Selene know I was victorious, and the others in the pack replied back.

Padding through the forest, I spotted the silver light again. Knowing who it was, I followed her through the underbrush and into one of the clearings. She stood there; her hands folded in front of her as she waited for me.

Shifting back to human form, she clothed me as I came up to her, kneeling and baring my neck to her in submission, I waited for her to say something. Selene lifted my head, bringing my attention to her face. She smiled at me as she motioned for me to rise.

Rising to my feet, I stood before her. Her hands went to my upper arms, giving them a gentle squeeze before she placed a hand on the side of my face. "I knew you could do it, Nolen. You've brought three packs together that would not have been if you were not alpha. I am so proud of you, Nolen. You have exceeded my expectations, and I have gifts for you."

"I'm glad that this is all over. My pack will be able to rest easy now that Wade is gone. They will be able to get their lives back together again." A familiar scent wafted between us; the adrenaline from my fight must have been playing games with my mind. There was no way that his scent could be here on this plane.

"There is someone who wants to speak with you, Nolen." I gave Selene a curious glance as she motioned to her right. My heart dropped when my eyes landed on my brother, who stood there with his goofy smile on his face. I turned my attention to Selene, and she nodded, motioning again to go to him.

Making my way forward to him, I realized that he had no physical form, and he was whole. I could feel the tears falling down my cheeks of their own accord. Every time I was near the Moon Goddess, I became emotional. When I got to him, I no longer had to gaze up, we were the same height, and we could now pass for twins. "Archer?"

"Yeah, little bro. You've grown into a badass alpha." His voice sounded the same other than the wispy undertone. I tried to touch his arm, but my hand went through him. Tears streamed faster down my face. The person I admired more than anyone stood before me, telling me I was a badass when I felt anything but at the moment.

"I've missed you so much, so has mother and dad. The pack misses you," I told him as I sat down in the grass. He sat with me, gazing into my eyes. It felt so surreal staring at him in this form.

"I know you, mom, and dad miss me. The pack misses me a tiny bit, but they have faith in you, little brother. You are their alpha, and I couldn't be more proud of what you have accomplished. Your mate is feisty." He chuckled as he mentioned Amora. I chuckled as well as I fiddled with a blade of grass.

"She will definitely keep me on my toes. But I wouldn't trade her for anyone." Glancing up from the sliver of green in my hands I was now tying in on itself. Archer's grin made me snort to myself. Sarge whimpered inside my head, wanting to talk with him as well.

"Sarge has been taking care of you. You released him early, which means you were always going to be stronger than me." I shook my head at his words; there was no way that I would be anywhere near as strong as him. He would always be the strongest in my eyes, even if someone wanted to argue differently.

"Archer, I don't know what to do about the rest of the Dolostone pack. How do I know who to trust? I'm sorry I couldn't protect Axel." My gaze went to my lap. I needed guidance and didn't know who else to ask than the most intelligent person I ever knew. His cool astral form passed through my shoulder, bringing my attention back to him.

"Nolen, they are part of your pack now. Most of the Dolostone wolves didn't like Alpha Wade, and deep down, you understand why. This was your destiny, and it has only just begun. Just remember that I'm always with you even when I'm not physically. I'm glad Sarge got a second chance. He deserved it. Axel is fine now, he is with us. I'm glad you got to see him at his best before he went." Tears filled his eyes at the mention of our wolf, and I decided that he needed to see him just as much as me.

Hey, bud, you want to take over? Spend some time with Archer? I thought to Sarge. His tail beat excitedly, and I let the massive animal have control. He shifted, landing on all four paws in one fluid motion, before he sat in front of my brother, his tongue hanging out like a dog. *"Hey, there, big guy. It's kinda weird seeing you like this. You keeping my brother safe?" His hand came down on reflex, but this time didn't go through Sarge but caressed his head like a pet. Sarge nudged his hand before he licked it and stood bumping his head into Archer's chest. Archer chuckled and massaged both Sarge's ears. I would never let anything happen to Nolen, Archer. I promised you when I came back I would protect him.*

"I appreciate that you did, Sarge, and I'm so glad that you have each other. Help him protect the pack and y'all's mate. Take care of each other." Archer gazed into our eyes as he started to fade away back from where he came. Selene smiled at Sarge and vanished as well. I couldn't help but cry, which made Sarge lift his head, and a sorrowful howl escaped his mouth, telling the world our sorrow as other howls rang out after ours.

CHAPTER TWENTY-THREE: CHANGING MINDS

Reaching the edge of the woods, I stopped to gaze upon the scene before me. Bodies littered the land as pack members went around checking for the living. I went forward, stepping over the bodies that no longer carried life. My eyes searched for my mate to ensure she was okay since I had not been by her side the entire time but couldn't find her in the field. Trotting by a few pack members, they bowed their heads before resuming what they had been doing. As I made my way to the pack's center, more pack members surrounded me and bowed their heads. When I made it to the packhouse, my parents stood on the steps, along with Lucas and Amora. Warrior wolves surrounded Dolostone members. I stared at them; some of them were young kids, and probably hadn't even possessed their wolves for more than a year. They were scared, their eyes wide as saucers as they sat there staring at Sarge as I walked by them.

I shifted, and Amora ran down the steps, jumping into my arms. Hugging her tighter to me, I was fully aware I was naked and that just her touch turned me on. The anxiety that ran through me dissipated as soon as she touched me. Her scent calmed me more than she would ever know; nuzzling into her mark, I walked up the stairs with her in my arms. "I missed you so much."

"Nolen, I've been here the entire time." Amora kissed my mark with a giggle, causing me to shiver. I placed her down on her feet in front of me. My mother brought me some shorts, which I put on and gave my mother a hug. Breaking the embrace, I gazed upon her healing face. The wolf that did this to her was immediately executed by my father once Harley broke him out of the dungeon.

"I'm fine, Nolen. Let's send these people to bed. Things can be cleaned up later." My mother's hand rested on my cheek as she gazed into my eyes. Grinning at her, I nodded and turned to my pack that had gathered around the pack steps.

"Pack members, sleep for the rest of the night. Once it is light, we will all come out to pick up the dead. In three days, we will hold a funeral for the wolves lost in this battle, along with those who have yet to have their funeral. Dolostone wolves that surrendered, for the time being, will go down to our dungeons. I promise that no harm or maltreatment will befall you." Nodding to the warrior wolves, they stood the Dolostone wolves up and led them to the dungeon. The younger wolves seemed scared as they followed my warriors. The older ones glared at me. I knew what they thought; they figured I was lying, something they were most likely used to.

I motioned for one of the omegas to come to me. He came up to me and bowed his head before he lifted his to gaze at me. "Yes, sir?"

"Make sure that the Dolostone wolves are given food and drink. We are not like them. We will not be tyrants." I placed a hand on the boy's shoulder and motioned him on as a few other wolves followed him. The other wolves looked on as they tramped after them. A young child came up to me and grabbed hold of my hand. Kneeling down at the pup before me, brushing back her matted hair behind her ear, her tiny little body a skeleton with flesh. "What is it, sweetheart?"

"I'm hungry too," her tiny voice rang out, pulling on my heartstrings. I grabbed her up just as her mother ran up franticly to the small child in my arms. The she-wolf bowed her head and reached for the child.

"I'm very sorry, Alpha. She won't disturb you any longer." Her voice held fear in it as she spoke to me. I would never harm a pup, much less one that was hungry.

"She is not disturbing me. Everyone, come with me. We will find you something to eat so that you can go to bed with some food in your bellies." I turned from the mother with her pup in my arms and walked into the packhouse. Amora followed me, along with my mother and Lucas.

I went into the kitchen, and a few omegas were already there, getting pitchers of water and sandwiches ready for the surrendered wolves. They glanced over at me and then between themselves. I sat the pup on the island and began to help the omegas make the food. Amora stood in the doorway, a slight grin on her lips. "Go take these to the packs in the dining hall. It's not going to be much, but it will help for tonight."

Amora nodded and left to do as I asked. The pup sat watching me as I made her half of a sandwich. Grabbing a napkin, I put it on the paper towel and handed it to the pup, who hungrily bit into the sandwich.

Chuckling, I stayed in the kitchen to help with the food, making sure everyone had something to eat. Once we were finished, another set of omegas came in and got the food for the Dolostone wolves. I found the head kitchen staff and went up to her. She bared her neck before standing straight to gaze at me. "Can I help you, sir?"

"Yes, can you write me a list of items we are out of, I will make sure everything gets replenished." The she-wolf glanced up at me as she thought of what to say next.

"Sir, we haven't possessed much since you left. I don't know what the Dolostone Alpha did while he was here, so I don't know if we have the funds." She fiddled with her hands on her apron, waiting for me to respond. Would he have been able to hack into the pack accounts? I didn't leave any passwords or anything in the office or my room, and the only other one that would know them would've been Axel.

"Okay. Well, let me get back to you. Take a break, eat some food, and I'll send someone to the city to obtain the food. I'm sorry this has happened to all of you." There was nothing more I could do at the moment other than apologize for not taking care of them like I should've. I let my pack down, but I would not let them go hungry again. That was a promise.

Turning, I noticed that the little pup had fallen asleep on the island; picking her up, I made my way to the dining hall and bumped into Sawyer. I glanced at the only best friend I possessed other than Archer and clapped him on the shoulder. "Looks like your hands are full. Anything you want me to help with?"

"No, I'm taking her to her mother, and then I'm going to my office to see if the pack accounts are ruined. This pack has not possessed anything good to eat since I left, and I feel guilty about it." Shaking my head and strolling past him, Sawyer fell into step with me as we entered the dining room. I found the pup's mother and handed her off to her. She smiled at me and turned to the other she-wolves at her table.

The room was almost empty as wolves got up to leave. Even though we won this war, they looked defeated, and I hated that. I turned to Sawyer and motioned for him to follow me. We went into the room, and it looked as if it had been trashed. Filing cabinets were tipped over and desk drawers were pulled out. Sighing, I set to work picking up all the papers that were tossed around the room.

Sawyer helped pick up the cabinets and papers, placing the documents on the desk. Luckily the computer was not smashed up, and I rebooted it to see if I could find out about the pack funds. Sawyer plopped down in the torn-up seat, glancing around the room. "That alpha tried to find something in here."

"Yeah, I think he was trying to find the code for the pack funds. The only other one who would've known them was Axel, and he killed him," I told him as I began putting in all the information to login into the accounts. After several attempts and verification on my part, I got in. To my surprise, all the funds were there, plus more since the revenue from our businesses was credited to the pack's accounts.

"Well? Are they all there?" Sawyer leaned forward as he stared at me. I nodded my head and glanced over at him with a smile. This would help the pack a lot. I logged off and stood. The papers would wait to be refiled when I possessed more time. Right now, I needed to let the head omega know that we could send a group to town to grab the groceries.

The door to the office opened, and my dad walked in with my mother. They stopped beside Sawyer and glanced around the office, I could tell he was getting angry at the state of the room, and I couldn't blame him. "Yes, father?"

"What happened in here?" He motioned around the room as he gazed at me. Sawyer cocked an eye at me, and I just shook my head. Coming around the desk, I came to my dad.

"It seems after Wade took the pack and put you and mother in the dungeons, he tried to find the account codes. The only other person who knew was Axel, and I of course." He seemed to relax and then turned to my mother. He nodded and pulled me into a hug, shaking slightly, and I thought I heard a sob. Pulling away from him, I tilted my head in curiosity. My father never cried. Ever.

"We thought we lost you. They told us he killed you. Daylen said you'd been torn apart in the Alpha challenge. I couldn't understand why until I couldn't mind link him. He had betrayed the pack and had helped starve the rest. Some of the pack had mates within the Dolostone pack, which caused some uproar. Most of the pack would not concede to his rule, so they were given less food. Your mother never believed that you were gone. She said that she would've felt it. Like she did when Archer went." He glanced over to my mother, caressing her cheek with his hand. If there was one thing I knew about my father, it was that he loved my mother more than anything in this world. She was his world; he would die for her.

"I thought I would never come back to you both, back to the pack. But I had a few people to help me along the way. Without them, I couldn't have become what I am today. I have to talk to the lead omega about the kitchen. We need food for the pack." I gave my mother a quick hug and then went past them, Sawyer behind me as we left.

Amora strolled up to me; she had changed into some shorts and a tank top. I licked my lips, this girl was my Achilles heel, but I wouldn't have it any other way. Her hand slid over my chest when she reached me, causing me to shiver under her touch. My hand went to both sides of her face, bringing her gaze to mine. "Are you heading to bed?"

"Yes. When will you be up?" Those beautiful amber eyes searched mine. As we stood there in the hall, the packhouse had become quiet. Her tongue flicked out, wetting her lips. I loved it when she unintentionally turned me on.

"I have to tell the head kitchen omega that we can send someone to replenish the food. Then I'll be up." Pulling her into a hug, I kissed her mark before bringing her lips to mine. She broke the kiss, her fingers coming up to touch her lips. I noticed her eyes glance behind me and realized she had finally spotted Sawyer.

"Well, don't take too long, Alpha." Her eyes were filled with lust as she ran her fingers over my mark before she turned and sauntered away from me, her hips swaying back and forth. Running a hand down my face, I continued forward with Sawyer chuckling behind me.

The head omega was still in the kitchen, and when she spotted Sawyer and me, she bared her neck before straightening back up. She glanced between us, and I thought she was afraid. "Make a list of what all is needed, and a group of people will go get the food. If you need anything for the kitchen or anything else, just put it on the list."

"Oh, thank you, Alpha! Now we might be able to fatten some of these kids up." She quickly turned around and started making a list. I went out of the room with Sawyer and up the stairs to the bedrooms. I felt drained after everything, but I was glad that this was all over.

"So, how's Danika?" I turned to Sawyer before he went to his room.

"She's doing okay. Getting more pregnant as the days go by. I'm nervous that things are going to change between us. I mean, she will have her hands full with a pup from my genes. I was a handful when I was a pup." He ran his hand over his face and through his hair. I could tell he was nervous; hell, I'd be the same way. Bringing my hand to his shoulder, I squeezed it.

"Brother, I think every first-time parent is nervous. But you will be fine." Sawyer grinned at me and nodded, pulling me into a hug before he opened the door to go in.

Going over to my door, I could smell Amora already in there. Entering the room, I realized that she was fast asleep. Smiling to myself, I slid into bed with her, not worrying about a shower since my body was exhausted and I realized I wouldn't have been able to take a shower. Snuggling up close to her, I wrapped my arms around her body and fell asleep.

)))) ▶ 🐺 ◀ (((((

My body felt like a boulder as I peeled open my eyes and turned over onto my back. Finally adjusting to the blaring light, I realized that Amora was not in bed with me. She hadn't been in the room for some time now. Her scent had faded out the door, telling me she had left me here to sleep.

Throwing my legs over the side of the bed, I stretched out all the muscles in my body. Standing, I went to the bathroom and took a quick shower after I spotted the time. Drying off, I put on some clean clothes and went out of the room. Making my way down the stairs, I found that a few omegas had started to clean up the packhouse.

Pack members were bringing in crates of food, everyone had a bounce in their step. I found Amora outside giving directions to other pack members. She had always been a leader, and she would be my greatest asset. Grinning, I went up to her and turned her to face me. "Nolen! About time you got up! I was about to tell Lucas to go up and throw you out of bed."

"You wouldn't have done that," I laughed, cocking an eyebrow at her and then pecking her lips in front of everyone nearby. A few teenagers wolf-whistled, and I couldn't help but grin wider. Breaking the kiss, I glanced around at all the members helping to get things back to normal.

"Where is Lucas, by the way? I need him and Sawyer with me to go to the dungeons." I brushed a lock of hair behind her ear. She patted me on the chest and pointed over to the side of the house. Placing a kiss on the top of her head, I headed over to the two male wolves.

"Hey, guys, let's make our way to the dungeons and find out what we can do with the Dolostone wolves." They both nodded and followed me to the dungeons. Two guards stood by the doorway, ensuring no one came in unless to give the Dolostone wolves food and drink. I nodded to them and went inside with Sawyer and Lucas behind me.

The dungeon was underground so not much light filtered in unless the door was open, or the lights were on. Once we reached the bottom of the stairs, the cells surrounded us in a circular formation. The older wolves sat at the back of the cells while the younger ones sat in the middle. When they all realized who I was, the scent of fear coming off the younger wolves was staggering. "None of you have anything to fear. I have only come to talk."

An older male came up to the cell bars; this wolf had seen many things over the years he had been on this earth. The scars alone on his face and torso told a thousand words. He lazily draped his hands through the bars as he sized all three of us up. "That is what you alphas always say to get prisoners to comply with you. What is it that you want with us?"

Lucas started to confront him, but I held out my hand to stop him and shook my head. Crossing my arms over my chest, I went forward to stand face to face with the older wolf. Allowing my gaze to sweep over his body before bringing my eyes back to his face. "Listen, I'm not here to harm anyone of you. That is not my style and never will be. Your alpha has passed on, and I've come; well, we both have come to see if any of you would like to join our packs. If not, you will be rogue unless someone from another pack will take you in. What is your name, sir?"

The older wolf seemed taken aback at my statement and question. We both stared at each other for a few moments as the mumbling from the other wolves came from the other cells. He stepped back, and his gaze went to both Sawyer and Lucas. The door to the dungeon opened, and Fin's scent carried down on the breeze from the open door. Fin came up beside me and stared at the older wolf as he crossed his arms over his chest. "Harlen, is there a reason you're looking a gift horse in the mouth?"

"Fin! What are you doing here? I thought you had been put to death!" The old wolf came back up to the bars, reaching his hand to Fin. Fin grabbed hold of the old man's hand and shook it.

"Harlen, you realize these young pups need to go with one of these alphas. There's no reason why you should go rogue after everything you and they have been through. Rogue is not for the faint of heart." Harlen glanced over to Sawyer and me and then back to Fin. I could tell these two knew each other from a long time ago. The way the old man gazed at Fin made me think he had once been a part of Fin's pack.

"Why don't you return as Alpha of Dolostone? You understand we would be better as three packs instead of two," the old man said, and I realized that he had been part of his pack. But had he always been Dolostone, or had he been part of a pack that was taken over by Alpha Wade? I turned to Fin and glanced at him; his face was stoic, as always, showing nothing to give me a clue about what was going on.

"That would not be a good idea. I've been rogue way too long to be an alpha now." He cocked an eyebrow at Harlen when the old man scoffed and then started to pace. The air in the room grew tense as the two of them kept silent. These two had history, and I didn't know if I wanted to be here when that history came out to play.

Fin turned to leave and was halfway to the stairs when the old man hit the bars, rattling the iron cage. Fin turned to him, a lazy expression on his face. "You know you are the rightful alpha of that pack! Your uncle was never meant to have it!"

CHAPTER TWENTY-FOUR: REBUILDING

What took Wade a few weeks to demolish took me a couple of years to rebuild. The pups that had been raised under him took a while to trust that I wouldn't harm them. Everything was a learning curve for everyone, including me.

I took the oath of the alpha a few days after we held the massive funeral for all the wolves lost in battle. Amora took her place beside me as Luna; she'd been born for this just like I was. Lucas became my beta, and Hannah and Harley took over the Gamma position.

The Delta position was still up in the air as Daylen's mate ran after she found out he had been caught and was sentenced to death for war crimes. I didn't know where she was, but I realized she wouldn't be with the Quartzite pack or the Dolostone pack. She might have gone back to her original pack before she'd met Daylen.

Fin finally conceded to be Alpha of the Dolostone pack. Which made me feel safer he was able to take over, we could have split them up between mine and Sawyer's pack, but this felt right. Like something Selene would have wanted. To bring the packs back in harmony.

Old man Harlen had been Fin's father's beta and now acting Beta until his daughter came of age. Fin had a whole lot to fix as well, and Sawyer and I helped with that since his uncle depleted the packs' funds. He tried to dismiss our help, but there would've been no way he would be able to get out of the debt that his uncle had forced the pack into.

The lands my father and Wade had disputed about now became a neutral place for all the packs to gather. We built a school for the pups of all the packs to attend. Calling the school Tri-Cairn since it resided between all three packs. Can you believe that Olli decided he would be one of the teachers there? I laughed at the thought when he told me, but thinking back to when he helped me through those weeks as a rogue, I knew he would be a good one.

Today, I sat at my desk working through all the files and revenue for the pack. It was a beautiful sunny day, and the warmth from the sun called my name. Sarge snorted; he'd seemed agitated the entire morning. Which, in turn, made me distracted. *What is your deal this morning?*

Something feels off with mate. She and Kulai are hiding something. The massive animal paced in my head, his tail tucked tightly against himself. As much as I needed to finish this paperwork, there would be no way with Sarge acting like this that I would be able to get anything done. Standing, I stretched out the hours of unused muscle and headed for the door.

Leaving the office, I stood in the hallway, sniffing out my Luna's scent. The packhouse was unusually quiet, and that bothered me even more. I set off down the hall to the front part of the house; Sarge was at attention inside my head.

Her scent called to me but not from upstairs in our bedroom. Strolling out onto the front steps, I saw her walking down the drive into the woods with Hannah. It was never good when those two were together, so I decided to follow them. For one, she shouldn't be going into the woods in her condition, and two... I couldn't think of a two at the moment.

We had been blessed by the goddess, and she carried twins. The pack doctor had told her she needed to stay off her feet. But what was he going to do when even I couldn't make her do anything she didn't want to, and I was Alpha. When she told me she was pregnant, I thought I would vomit, because I was not prepared for that; I was still trying to bring this pack back to whole. And then, when the doc said it was twins, I fought to keep myself from passing out.

That's when he put her on bed rest, but that Luna of mine would not stay in her room. She has always been stubborn and would do what she wanted anyway. The good thing was Hannah always followed her around, which made me feel a little better knowing someone would be with her if something was to happen.

Following them, I snuck into the woods, using my sense of smell to guide me since they had been further ahead of me. The closer I came to the edge of the woods, the more I started to recognize the other wolves' scents. What was Amora doing?

"SURPRISE!!!"

I stood at the edge of the woods, stumped. What was today? Did I miss something? All of my pack and some of Sawyer's came as well, along with Sawyer and Danika and their pups. Amora came up to me, a smile on her face. I was still trying to figure out what this was all about.

"What is all of this?"

Amora giggled when she got to me, straightening my hair and pulling out the twigs that had gotten tangled in it. Her hands came to my face and brought my attention to her smile growing as she stared at me. "Nolen, it's your birthday!! You've been working so much you have forgotten it."

Holy shit! It's my birthday; how could I have forgotten today? And everyone had let me forget too. I had been in my office all morning, but Amora had brought me in breakfast like normal. But no, thinking about it now, I recalled she'd had my favorite things on the plate and had placed a kiss on my lips a little longer than expected. Glancing down at my beautiful mate, I smiled and then crashed my lips to hers. Wolf-whistles sounded from behind her. I broke the kiss to let her breathe and then glanced over the crowd of wolves in the clearing. "Thank you all for all of this! It has been a tough time rebuilding and getting things back to normal. A lot of that was you all."

The crowd cheered, and Sawyer and Danika came up to us. While the rest of the wolves began to mingle with the others. I pulled Sawyer into a hug and then gave Danika a brief one. "Thank you both for coming. It's still crazy that wolves come to my parties now."

"Man, you saved them from a tyrant. They know you are the real deal and that you are a badass." Sawyer clapped his hand on my shoulder as Danika and Amora walked off. Their pups, a girl and a boy, played with the other pups in the clearing. They were a year apart and feisty as hell but mine would be together, which meant I would have double the trouble from the start.

"How do you do it, man? I mean, when she told me she was pregnant, I about had a nervous breakdown, but when doc told us there would be two, I thought this couldn't be happening." I glanced over at him from the corner of my eye and saw him chuckling. He turned to me and met my gaze, his expression serious this time.

"Well, it's pretty easy. I mean, Danika had most of the job when they were younger. They wouldn't come to me, always wanting their momma, but when Zac started getting older, he started wanting me more. I tried to help her, but they just didn't want me." Sawyer shrugged as we observed them all playing. One day, mine would be out there running around, bossing all the other pups around. Two mean little boys running the pack together when they come of age. Naw, they wouldn't be mean, but they wouldn't be bullied like me. I'd never let them act like a tyrant, though, that was not how this pack was run.

"With Amora, she'll have two to deal with; I can't let her do all the work. That would drain her." I shook my head at Sawyer as he chuckled at me. But he didn't say anything more as we watched everyone enjoy themselves at the party.

))))) 🐺 (((((

The doors to my office opened, and Amora waddled in. I sat there watching her as she came up to me and leaned up against my desk. Yes, I said waddle, but I say it with love because Amora is even more beautiful now that she is round with my children than she ever was. She gazed at me, and I cocked an eyebrow at her. "What can I do you for Luna?"

"Nothing. Kulai is pacing, and I'm not feeling too well either. The little ones are not moving as much, and my belly is tight." Amora rubbed her stomach with both her hands. It'd been two weeks since my birthday, and Amora neared her due date. I stood from my chair and reached for my mate. Her stomach was as hard as a rock; small kicks from my boys and quivers in her stomach raced downward.

"Have you been to the pack doctor? This might be the start of labor." I ran my hands over her stomach, and when she moaned, I tried to keep from losing it. Her fingers traced the outline of my tricep, down the bicep, to my forearm.

"No, I've bothered him so much since last week. I don't want to bother him anymore. Mhmm." Her eyes squeezed shut, and her stomach tightened. When they opened again, Kulai's eye color showed through. Her hand rested on my chest; I could sense the pressure through her thoughts.

"Alright, Amora, we are going to the doctor. This is intense even for me." I tried to pick her up, but she pushed into my chest. Alright, well, if she wouldn't let me take her to him, I'd bring him to her. *Oscar, get down here now! My office, I think she's in labor this time.*

Be right there, Alpha.

I felt the next contraction, and damn if it wasn't even more intense than the last one. Amora started to sweat, and I knew this was not going to be good if she birthed these pups in my office. Taking her chin in my hand, I brought her attention up to me. "Listen, my love, we need to take you to the doc. This seems to be different than the other times."

She gave me a pained look, and that's when her water broke. Oscar rushed in just as she slumped over in pain, and it took everything in me to keep from following her. The pack doctor came up to us and started to assess her. He glanced up at me after he looked her over. "We need to take her to the ward. These pups are on their way."

I grabbed Amora up and carried her bridal style behind Oscar. Another contraction hit her harder than the other. We made it to the ward, and I placed her on one of the beds, sliding down her shorts and panties. Nurses came up to us and pushed her into a labor and delivery room as Oscar gloved up and put on some type of paper gown.

He motioned me to follow him. We both walked into the room where the nurses had already hooked her up to monitors and dressed her in a gown. I could detect each contraction getting worse as I made my way to her side. Taking hold of her hand, she squeezed, and I placed a soft kiss on the back. She turned her gaze on me as another contraction took hold; her grip tightened as well. "Nolen, I can't do this."

I gazed into her amber eyes that happened to be full of tears as the next contraction gripped her. A tear fell from my eye and down my cheek. Using my other hand, I wiped away her tears and stared at her, keeping her eyes connected to mine. "But you can, Amora. You are strong and beautiful. I know you can bring these boys into the world."

She chuckled at that. We hadn't found out what the pups were going to be, but she always told me that they were going to be girls, that she just knew. Some part of me thought they were girls as well, but a man could hope for boys, right? Amora shook her head, the sweat drenching her hair; a nurse pulled it up out of her face, fastening it into a bun. "Doctor, she is four centimeters, almost five."

Oscar nodded as all the nurses in the room made sure everything was in order before leaving. He came up to her monitors, checking the babies' heartbeats along with Amora's. Turning from the machines, he glanced between us as he pulled off his gloves. "She has five more centimeters before she can start to push. Luna, if you want an epidural, we can place that now, but any later, and the babies will have to be born without it."

Amora looked at me, and I just shrugged. This would be up to her; I wasn't going to make this decision for her. Amora glanced back to Oscar and shook her head. As much as the pain was starting to become worse, I supported her in whatever she wanted. "Alright, Luna, a nurse will be in every few minutes to see how you are progressing. I believe in the next hour these pups will be in your arms."

"Thank you, Oscar." He glanced over at me and nodded before he turned away and left the room. Turning to Amora, she had leaned back into the bed, her eyes closed as she regulated her breathing. I lifted my hand and wiped some of the sweat that was on her forehead off; her eyes snapped open at my touch, and she smiled when our eyes met.

"You remember when you came to our pack? You were the most handsome wolf I'd ever seen, well, besides my dad." Amora grinned at me; I could still remember her hiding behind her mother's skirts as she peered around them to stare at me. Chuckling, I nodded and placed a kiss on her forehead while I caressed her cheek with my hand.

"You are one amazing person. I could never forget coming to your pack; my life changed so much when I lived there." Another contraction hit her, making her bite her lower lip, and then it was gone. They came quicker than before because as soon as that one hit, another came right after it. A nurse came and pulled on some gloves; she lifted the sheet and checked her. The blonde she-wolf grinned at us as she took off the gloves.

"You're getting closer, Luna. One of them is already dropped. I'm going to grab Dr. Oscar, and we will be back in to have you start pushing." We both nodded as the woman left to go collect Oscar. I gave Amora a kiss on her lips and then on the back of the hand that I was holding. Oscar and two nurses came in; he had on the paper gown and more gloves. They placed her feet in the stirrups, and Oscar checked her himself. *He better be glad he is the doctor; otherwise, his hand would be detached from his arm.* I chuckled to myself at Sarge's response to Oscar touching Amora, I mean, I didn't like it either, but that was what needed to happen. Oscar glanced up to the both of us and nodded.

"Alright, Luna. It's time to push."

))) 🐺 ((((

Amora lay in the bed as she rested from the two-hour-long birth of our girls. Yes, I had twin girls. They were not identical twins, so that helped me a lot. I held my girls against my bare chest, giving them warmth and skin-to-skin contact. Sarge lay on his stomach, his head resting on his massive paws as his tail swept the ground. They completed the missing link in my and Amora's family. They were beautiful; I couldn't keep my eyes off them. They both had their mother's hair, but one had my blue eyes, and the other had Amora's eyes.

The door cracked open, and my mother and father came in quietly, followed by Sawyer, Danika, and Amora's parents. Their smiles made me grin as my mom and Amora's mom gave each other an excited glance before pushing the others out of the way. They both sat on either side of me, softly touching the girls' hair, making them snuggle further into me. My mother caressed my cheek and placed a quick kiss on my daughter's head. "What did you and Amora decide to name them?"

I grinned, realizing that this was my moment to prank them all. I leaned up with the girls in my arms, repositioning myself to make myself comfortable again. Glancing around the room, I sighed. "Well, I decided that since Amora has been out since the last babe was born that we are going to name them Dave and Hank."

Sawyer tried to keep from laughing, and Danika's jaw had dropped. My mother and Amora's looked at me like I had two heads. I heard a sigh from Amora's bed and the rustle of sheets as she sat up in bed. "I hope that you all realize that he is joking. Their names are Rosalind and Everleigh."

The breaths from the people in the room made me laugh out loud, waking up the girls in my arms, which made them start to cry. Amora motioned for me to bring them to her, and I got up, handing her Rosalind and letting her latch the first baby and then helping her get Everleigh latched. The sounds of their swallowing made my heart soar, my little girls were strong, and they would be the best Alphas this pack would ever have.

CHAPTER TWENTY-FIVE: REMEMBRANCE

AMORA

Today was going to be hard after being with him for so many years. I sat in the room we shared for the last seventy years, thinking about all the times we enjoyed together, only to outlast him. The room was colder now that his soul went to be with Selene. I had experienced death before with my parents and then Nolen's, but this happened to be the other part of my soul that had been ripped from me. The very essence of my being had been torn from me in one go.

He went peacefully to our Goddess during the night. I had woken with a start as I felt something pull away from me, and when I turned to him, he lay there as still as a statue. I tried to wake him up, shake him to bring him back to me, and then when all that failed, I mind linked the pack doctor. But it was too late; he was already gone.

In the distance, I could see them building the pyre he would be placed upon later tonight. To send his body back to our mother, Selene. I couldn't force myself to go down to the great hall to see him; I couldn't sit there and grieve in a place where his spirit no longer resided. *Selene, why take him before me? Why couldn't we have left together?*

Nolen had been a fantastic alpha to the pack that had bullied and belittled him in his younger years. He never took vengeance on them, and he never treated them any different than what he treated the others. The pack prospered under him and became one of the bigger packs in the Cairn land. The rest of the Alphas, younger and older alike, looked up to him.

He was indeed a Goddess sent gift. Nolen happened to be an amazing father to our two little girls. Even though I knew he wanted boys, he treated those girls like they came from royalty. Rosalind turned out to be the tomboy, and Everleigh was the little girlygirl, but they were strong-willed and put Nolen through his paces as they grew. He taught them to be strong, to stand up for themselves, and to always protect each other because, in the end, they would be the leaders of this pack.

I missed him so much. My daughters had been in and out of my room trying to make me eat. Eating hadn't been too appealing to me over the last few days. Plates of food sat abandoned on the small table in the room along with a pitcher of water which hadn't been touched.

The table where we'd enjoyed our first dinner as a mated pair and the table where I had told him we were going to be parents. I couldn't sit there ever again; that was our table. So, now I sat here on the window seat, waiting for when they came up to take me to the pyre to watch his physical form be taken away from me as well.

Leaning my head back against the wall, I closed my eyes. How would I be able to travel this life without him? He would be so upset with me right now with the thoughts that raced through my mind. Nolen never allowed me to think negative thoughts, he always kept me positive, even when he wasn't himself. Like when he thought he was being a terrible father when he had to punish the girls after they had left the pack lands without telling anyone.

My reflection stared back at me. For being ninety years old, I didn't look my age. I could probably still pass for forty, which made this so much harder. The door to my room opened again and Rosalind came in. I sighed at my excitement in thinking it would have been Nolen. Coming back to me after being out talking with other alphas. "Hey, Momma, can I get you anything?"

I shook my head and turned away from her, waiting for her to close the door and leave. Rosalind strolled up to me and sat on the ground beside the window seat, laying her head on my lap. Glancing down, Nolen's eyes stared up at me with tears running down his daughter's face. I began humming while I stroked her hair. Everleigh's footsteps brought her up to us and she curled up in the fetal position her head lying next to her sister's as I hummed their lullaby.

These two girls realized when I didn't feel right. They had let me be these last few days. Rosalind became alpha of our pack and Everleigh became the female beta to the Dolostone pack after Harlen's son turned of age. He happened to be a few years older than Everleigh, but I recognized that look when he laid eyes on her. Nolen told me it was the same gaze he had given me when he'd first shifted, and the only reason he knew was he saw it reflected in my eyes as well. So, we changed the law about not telling younger mates about the bond. But the law still stood about mating and marking until the other became old enough to sense the bond.

Nolen about lost it when he and Everleigh went over to the Dolostone pack and Harlen's son came up with Fin by his side and Tobey's wolf rose to the surface to try to claim Everleigh. Before he was able to get him back under control Nolen shifted into Sarge, bringing Tobey's wolf out and snarling, seeing another male near his mate. Everleigh was scared to death, seeing the other massive wolf in front of her father.

Oh! And when Rosalind's mate came for the twins' eighteenth birthday, that was exciting. He was the son of an alpha but he was the second born, like Nolen. He'd tried to make her submit, and when she didn't that's when both their wolves came out. It had been a downright brawl until Everleigh jumped into it. The poor guy didn't know what to do at that point.

They were both strong and independent women, just like their daddy taught them to be. These two were his world, and he made sure that they were very well-rounded. They could fight with the best and act like ladies right after. Just because they were girls, he never treated them like they couldn't take care of themselves, and he taught them to never take anyone's shit.

"Momma, you need to eat and drink, Daddy wouldn't want you to do this."

"Yeah, Momma. You know he wouldn't like this," my sweet Everleigh spoke up, dried tears on her cheeks. Her amber eyes pleading with me along with her sister's. I could never be half as sad with my girls with me, stroking their hair as they lay there with me on my window seat.

"I realize that, my sweet ones. What do you remember most about your daddy?" The girls glanced up at me and then at each other before turning their attention back to me. Small smiles crossed their lips as they gazed at me.

"I remember when he shifted into Sarge that one time when Chance kept messing with us after we told him to stop. He was so scared, and then when he snapped at him, and he ran off I could imagine his tail between his legs!"

"Oh, and what about the time when he rode us on his back through the woods. I couldn't wait to get my wolf to be able to fly like that!" Rosalind stood up to her full height as she grinned at me and her sister. Everleigh jumped up as well, excitement now on her face as tears ran down her cheeks.

"Oh, and the time we helped him surprise mom with her party! That was great! She didn't find out anything about it until the time it started!" Everleigh grabbed hold of Rosalind's upper arms as she and her sister swung around. They both laughed together. And it was nice to see them getting along. I stood from the window seat and grabbed the black dress from the closet.

Rosalind and Everleigh sat down on the window seat, a mixture of sad and happy tears. I went into the bathroom and changed into the dress. Pulling up my hair into simple updo, my eyes were red and my cheekbones showed more since food no longer called to me. Coming out, the girls must have cleared the table and left the room.

The pyre was almost complete just as the sun faded behind the trees. That sunset would be the last one he would be bodily here on this earth for. The last one we would be together for. A knock came upon the door and Sawyer walked in; his eyes no longer reflected the lively emotion they used to show. I not only lost a mate, but he lost a brother that he'd befriended long ago. "It's almost time, Amora."

I stared at him, tears welling up in his eyes as he gazed at me. The fearless alpha that I had grown up with and experienced the death of our parents with now displayed tears in his eyes for a man he called brother. I went to him, and he pulled me into a hug. I buried my face in his chest as he held me tight. "Let's head down then. The pack is waiting for us."

He nodded and we exited out of mine and Nolen's room, down the stairs that I had wandered for so many years, to the first floor and the pack of grieving wolves. A lot of them had grown up with Nolen in charge and didn't know anyone else other than our family. I patted each of them on the shoulder as Sawyer and I followed the wolves carrying Nolen to the pyre.

They'd dressed him in our burial robes, with his hands crossed over his chest. The yin and yang wolf tattoo had faded over the years but still reminded me of us and the way our wolves fit. Kulai grieved in her own way. She hadn't spoken to me since that night his soul was taken from him and me.

Olli, Fin, Markus, Harley, and Lucas carried him down through the pack square, everyone on the streets paying their respect to a fallen alpha.

The walk was long as we made our way to the wooden tower. Rosalind and Everleigh behind us with their mates, and their children behind them. Three packs followed behind us, paying their respect to an Alpha that the land didn't know it needed. An alpha that changed the view of so many leaders. I could only smile at the people he brought together, even though it happened to be his destiny, as the Moon Goddess Selene had written for his life.

They placed Nolen on the pyre, warrior wolves circling it holding torches, ready to send their alpha to be physically with our Goddess Selene. The elder went up in front of all of us as they circled around the pyre. He raised his hands to the sky, to the moon now above us.

"We are all here tonight to see this alpha off to be with Selene, our Goddess. To send him to be with the rest of his family. Tonight, might be a time of sorrow for us here, but he is rejoicing with his family that has gone before him. We will celebrate tonight the life and trials of one of our beloved alphas. He has definitely changed our world for the better."

The elder nodded to the warriors surrounding the pyre and they touched their flames to the wood, setting it ablaze in the night sky. The flames climbed the wood, engulfing the entire pyre, along with Nolen's body. The smell of human flesh and hair burned into my nostrils. I felt a small hand wrap around mine, and when I glanced down, I saw one of my grandsons. He was named after Nolen, and he looked just like him. Giving his little hand a squeeze, I smiled at him as tears streamed down my face.

This was his legacy.

ACKNOWLEDGMENT

I'd like to start out by thanking my two best friends, Kristin and Laura, who helped me when I felt like giving up. They have been my literal rocks. Then to the three authors who have been my inspiration since I met them and probably wouldn't have finished my first book if I hadn't.

To my lovely Editor Marni Macrae, who took my book and helped me take it to the next level and loved it from the start. Thank you so much for giving me more confidence!

Finally, to my husband. Who, through all the months of writing this one and others that are still not finished yet, has tried to be patient and uplifting as I went through the time I wanted to give up writing so many times. Thank you for being there.

ABOUT C. L. LEDFORD

C. L. Ledford was born in the city of Chattanooga, TN. Where she was raised by her grandparents, to be a strong and independent person. She became an avid reader at the age of eleven, when her fifth grade teacher gifted her the book, The Black Stallion. With this book her love of books grew.

In middle school she began to write what would be one of many books swirling around in her head. Silver Moon Kiss came to life with two chapters and multiple scenes before it was packed away and not thought of until after she had become an adult. C. L. Ledford writes in Paranormal Romance and Contemporary Romance. Her first published book The Second Alpha Heir released on June 14, 2022.

By this time she had moved to a little town called Ringgold, GA and married her husband where they raise their three children and five German Shorthair dogs. Along with her love of writing and reading, she also enjoys hunting behind her dogs.

ALSO BY C.L. LEDFORD

<u>Paranormal Romance</u>
The Second Alpha Heir
The Fallen Alpha
Silver Moon Kiss
Silver Moon Kiss: Becoming Alpha

<u>Contemporary Romance</u>
Raising the Stakes: A Dark CEO Romance
Craving the Taboo: A Dark Forbiddin Romance